Retold Classics

NOVELS

Frankenstein

Huckleberry Finn

The Red Badge
of Courage

The Scarlet Letter

A Tale of Two Cities

Treasure Island

ANTHOLOGIES

American Classics,
Volume 1

American Classics,
Volume 2

American Classics,
Volume 3

American Hauntings

British Classics

Classic Chillers

Edgar Allan Poe

Jack London

Mark Twain

O. Henry

World Classics

D0112398

The Retold Tales® Series features novels, short story
anthologies, and collections of myths and folktales.

Perfection Learning®

Writer

Wim Coleman
M.A.T. English and Education
Educational Writer and Novelist

Consultants

Rhonda Fey
Educational Consultant
Des Moines, Iowa

Gretchen Kauffman
Educational Consultant
Des Moines, Iowa

Dr. Jona Mann
Educational Consultant
Des Moines, Iowa

Lois Markham
Educational Writer
Beverly, Massachusetts

Retold Classics

by Mary Shelley

Perfection Learning®

Senior Editor
Marsha James

Editors
Christine Rempe LePorte

Cover Illustration
Mark Bischel

Inside Illustration
Frank McShane

Book Design
Dea Marks

For information contact
Perfection Learning® Corporation
1000 North Second Avenue, P.O. Box 500
Logan, Iowa 51546-0500.
Phone: 1-800-831-4190 • Fax: 1-800-543-2745
perfectionlearning.com

Paperback ISBN 1-5631-2266-9
Cover Craft® ISBN 0-7807-1701-5

15 16 17 PP 08 07 06

TABLE
OF CONTENTS

WELCOME TO THE RETOLD CLASSIC FRANKENSTEIN

Suspense, a haunting plot, and unforgettable characters are but a few of the elements that help make Mary Shelley's *Frankenstein* a classic work.

We call something a classic when it is so well loved that it is saved and passed down to new generations. Classics have been around for a long time, but they're not dusty or out-of-date. That's because they are brought back to life by each new person who reads and enjoys them.

Frankenstein is a novel written years ago that continues to entertain and influence readers today. The story offers exciting plots, important themes, fascinating characters, and powerful language. This is a story that many people have loved to read and share with one another.

RETOLD UPDATE

The *Retold Classic Frankenstein* is different from Shelley's original story in two ways.

- Some chapters have been omitted. Brief summaries are provided for these parts so you can follow the complete story.

- The language has been updated. All the colorful, gripping, or dramatic details of the original story are here. But longer sentences and paragraphs have been shortened or split up. And some old words have been replaced with modern language.

continued

You will also find these special features. A word list has been added at the beginning of each chapter. The list should make reading easier. Each word defined on the list is printed in dark type within that chapter of the novel. If you forget the meaning of a word while you're reading, just check the list to review the definition.

In addition, there is a map at the beginning of the book. This map identifies the different places mentioned in the novel.

You'll also see footnotes at the bottom of some pages. These notes identify people and places or explain words and ideas.

At the beginning of the book, you'll find a little information about Mary Shelley. These revealing facts will give you insight into her life and work.

One last word. If you feel compelled to read the entire story, we encourage you to locate an original version to get more of Shelley's rich characterization and exciting plot.

Now on to the novel. Remember, when you read this book, you bring the story back to life in today's world. We hope you'll discover why this novel has earned the right to be called a literary classic.

Mary Shelley

INSIGHTS INTO
MARY SHELLEY

(1797–1851)

From birth, Mary Wollstonecraft Shelley's life was one full of tragedy and sorrow. Her mother, the writer Mary Wollstonecraft, died just ten days after Mary's birth. A few years later, Mary's father, the writer William Godwin, remarried.

Mary's stepmother made no secret of her dislike for Mary. She constantly nagged and criticized her. Mary also felt that the new Mrs. Godwin favored her own daughter Claire over her.

Mary Shelley—who was born in London—received little formal education. But she was bright and clever and loved to read. Even as a child she wrote stories to amuse herself. She also delighted in listening to the famous writers who often visited her father.

One of the Godwins' frequent guests was the poet Percy Bysshe Shelley. Though Percy was married, he fell in love with Mary, and she with him. In 1814 the two ran away to the European mainland. Strangely enough, Mary's stepsister Claire went with them.

No one knows for sure why Claire accompanied Mary and Percy. Possibly the couple wanted someone to act as an interpreter.

But whatever the case, Mary was soon to regret taking Claire along. Claire was moody and complained about everything. She blamed Mary for anything that went wrong in her life. And sometimes it seemed that Claire spent more time with Percy than Mary did.

continued

Money was a problem for the threesome almost from the start. Though Percy came from a rich family, he never seemed to have enough money on hand. He gave most of his money to his deserted wife and daughter. He also loaned money to Mary's father.

As a result, the threesome had to struggle to survive. Nevertheless, they took great joy in their freedom to roam throughout Europe. Later, Mary wrote a book about their travels, entitled *History of a Six Weeks' Tour.*

It was money troubles that forced the three to return to England. Percy even had to beg some money from his wife in order to pay for the boat trip.

Percy and Mary settled in London to await the birth of their first child. The bothersome Claire stayed with them, and Mary was too polite to ask her to leave.

Tragedy struck when Mary's baby died shortly after birth. Mary's sadness and deep depression wore on Percy's nerves, and he spent a lot of time away from the house. Claire often went with him, a fact that didn't make Mary feel any better.

Happiness briefly returned when Claire went to live with some friends. Mary became pregnant again and gave birth to a boy, William. Parents and child lived in peace until Claire became "bored" and came back to live with them.

The summer of 1816 was an important period in Mary's writing career. She and Percy (and, of course, Claire) spent that summer in Switzerland. Lord Byron, another famous poet, lived nearby. He became a good friend of Percy and Mary.

One evening the group sat around a fireplace and read ghost stories together. Later that night, Lord Byron suggested that each of them write a ghost story.

At first, Mary had trouble coming up with a story. However, after a frightening nightmare and dreams of her dead baby coming back to life, the idea for *Frankenstein* was born.

Mary was nineteen when she wrote the novel. It began as a short story. When Percy read it, he encouraged Mary to build the story into a full-length novel. Mary took his suggestion.

While Mary worked on the book, a series of tragedies began to occur. First, Mary's half-sister Fanny committed suicide. Mary felt somewhat responsible, since Fanny had often complained of loneliness after Mary left home. Though depressed and grief-stricken, Mary continued writing.

In December 1816, Percy's wife Harriet also committed suicide. Percy and Mary married later that month. However, Percy failed to win custody of his and Harriet's two children. Seeing Percy's grief, Mary once again sank into a deep depression. However, the two were somewhat cheered when their daughter, Clara, was born.

In 1818 *Frankenstein* was published. But Mary wasn't aware of the novel's success at first. Percy's failing health forced them to Italy in search of a better climate.

Tragedy struck there when the Shelleys' two children became ill and died. This double blow was almost too much for Mary to bear. But Mary forced herself to continue writing, since that was her only comfort.

Indeed, Mary felt somewhat abandoned by her husband during her times of grief. For Percy could only ease his pain by going off alone and roaming the countryside.

Later, Mary gave birth to another son, Percy Florence. He was the only one of the Shelley children to survive into adulthood.

But unhappy fate wasn't yet through with the Shelleys. In 1822, Percy set off on a boating trip, despite Mary's strong fears that the venture would end in tragedy.

continued

While he was gone, Mary couldn't shake off her feeling of dread. She cried often, certain that something terrible was about to happen. Several days later, Percy's body was washed ashore—he had drowned.

Overcome with grief yet again, Mary took her son Percy and returned to England. To her surprise, Mary found she had become famous during the several years she was gone. *Frankenstein* was not only selling well—it had also been made into a popular play.

Mary—ever faithful to her husband—never married again. Instead, she spent her time collecting Percy's unpublished poems and preparing them for printing.

Mary continued her own writing too. But none of her works matched the popularity of *Frankenstein*. She died in London while working on biographies of both her husband and her father.

Other works by Mary Shelley
Falkner, novel
The Fortunes of Perkin Warbeck, novel
The Last Man, novel
Lodore , novel

Maps of Europe and Switzerland*

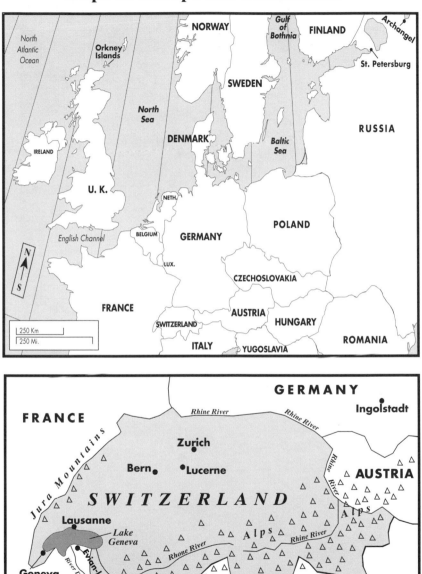

*The names and borders of some countries were different at the time
Frankenstein takes place.

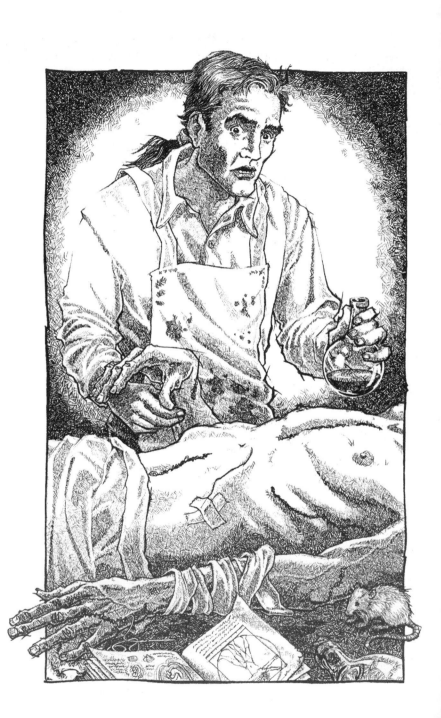

FRANKENSTEIN

by
Mary Shelley

Letter 1

To Mrs. Saville, England

St. Petersburg,[1] Dec. 11th, 17—

You will rejoice to hear what I have to say. My adventure has begun, and there has been no disaster. I arrived here yesterday, and my first task is to assure you—my dear sister—of my welfare. I know you are fearful about my venture. But I am more and more confident that my **enterprise** will be a success.

I am already far north of London. As I walk in the streets of Petersburg, I feel a cold northern breeze on my cheeks. This braces my nerves and fills me with delight.

Do you understand this feeling? This breeze has traveled from the regions towards which I am going. It

---

[1] St. Petersburg is a city in Russia on the Gulf of Finland. It was renamed Leningrad from 1924 to 1992.

gives me a foretaste of that icy climate. Inspired by this wind of promise, my daydreams become more eager and active.

I try to persuade myself that the pole is the seat of frost and bleakness. But still I see it as a place of beauty and delight. In my dreams, Margaret, the sun is forever visible there.[2] Its broad disk just skirts the horizon and spreads its everlasting splendor. With your permission, my sister, I will put some trust in earlier sailors. They say that snow and frost are driven away there. Sailing over a calm sea, we may be carried to a wonderful land.

This land will **surpass** the beauty of every region so far discovered on the inhabited globe. Its wildlife and features may be without compare. And the views of the heavenly bodies in those undiscovered stretches of land may also be unique.

What can't we expect in a country of eternal light? There I may discover the wondrous power which attracts the needle.[3] This power may control the movement of the stars. My voyage may forever make clear what has been puzzling about them.

I shall satisfy my eager curiosity by seeing a part of the world never before visited. I may tread on land that has never before felt the footprints of man.

These possibilities keep me going. They're enough to conquer all fear of danger or death. They urge me to begin this difficult voyage with joy. It is the joy a child feels when he takes off in a little boat, with his holiday companions, on an exploration up his native river.

But suppose all these ideas are false. Even then, you can't argue against the great good which I shall bring to mankind, to the last generation. Who knows? I may discover a shortcut to countries which require so many

---

[2] In fact, the sun sinks below the horizon at the pole during six months of every year.
[3] The needle of the compass points to "magnetic north." Sailors have long used the compass for direction.

months to reach now.[4] Or maybe I'll discover the secret of the magnet. These things can only be made possible by an undertaking such as mine.

These thoughts have rid me of any uneasiness I once had. I feel my heart glow with an enthusiasm which raises me to heaven. For nothing does so much to calm the mind as a firm purpose—a point on which the soul may fix its intellectual eye.

As you know, this expedition has been the favorite dream of my early years. I have read with **ardor** the accounts of various voyages. These voyages were made with the goal of arriving at the North Pacific Ocean through the seas which surround the pole. You may remember that a history of all these voyages made up the whole of our good Uncle Thomas' library.

My education was neglected, yet I was passionately fond of reading. I studied these volumes day and night. I got to know them very well. So it was with great regret that I learned—as a child—my father's dying command. He had forbidden my uncle to allow me to **embark** on a seafaring life.

My dreams of great sea adventures faded when I read the poets for the first time. Their words delighted my soul and lifted it to heaven. I became a poet and for one year lived in a paradise of my own creation. I imagined that I also might become as famous as Homer and Shakespeare.

You well know my failure. You know how heavy my disappointment was. But just at that time, I inherited my cousin's fortune. My thoughts were then turned again to the sea.

Six years have passed since I decided on my present undertaking. Even now, I can remember the exact time when I offered myself to this great enterprise. I began by toughening my body to hardship. I went with the whale

---

[4] To reach distant parts of Asia, English sailors then had to travel far to the south, rounding the southernmost points of Africa or South America. Walton—the letter writer—hopes to find a much shorter route by going through the Arctic Ocean.

fishers on several trips to the North Sea. I voluntarily
endured cold, hunger, thirst, and exhaustion.
During the day I often worked harder than the
common sailors. Then I spent my nights studying
mathematics and medicine. I also studied the branches of
physical science which might be most useful to a sea
adventurer.

Twice I actually hired myself as an under-mate in a
Greenland whaler[5] and proved myself with admiration. I
must admit I felt a little proud when my captain offered
me the second rank in the ship. He **earnestly** begged me
to remain. He considered my services of great value.

And now, dear Margaret, don't I deserve to
accomplish some great purpose? My life might have been
spent in ease and luxury. But I preferred glory to every
lure that wealth placed in my path. Oh, if only some
encouraging voice would answer yes to my question!

My courage and my determination are firm. But my
hopes are shaky, and my spirits are often depressed. I'm
about to set off on a long and difficult voyage. Its
emergencies will demand all my strength and courage.
Not only am I required to raise the spirits of others when
theirs are failing. But at the same time I must also keep
up my own spirits.

This is the most favorable period for traveling in
Russia. The Russians fly quickly over the snow in their
sledges.[6] The motion is pleasant. And in my opinion, it's
far more agreeable than that of an English stagecoach.

The cold is not extreme, if you are wrapped in furs—a
dress which I have already adopted. But there is a great
difference between walking the deck and remaining
seated motionless for hours. Sitting still provides no
exercise to prevent the blood from freezing in your veins.
I have no desire to lose my life on the post road between

---

[5] An under-mate is probably the same as a second mate, or the officer third in
   command after the captain. Greenland is the largest island in the world and
   lies to the northeast of North America.
[6] Sledges are sledlike vehicles used for traveling over snow.

St. Petersburg and Archangel.[7]

I shall leave for the latter town in two or three weeks. My intention is to hire a ship there. This can easily be done by paying the insurance for the owner. I can also hire as many sailors as I think necessary among those who are used to whale fishing.

I don't intend to sail until the month of June. And when shall I return? Ah, dear sister, how can I answer this question? If I succeed, many, many months, perhaps years, will pass before you and I may meet. If I fail, you will see me again soon, or never.

Farewell, my dear, excellent Margaret. Heaven shower down blessings on you and save me. I hope again to speak of how grateful I am for all your love and kindness.

Your affectionate brother,

R. Walton

---

[7] A post road is used to carry mail. Archangel is a port in northern Russia on the White Sea.

Letter 2 (Summary)

Walton next wrote from Archangel on March 28. He told his sister that he had hired a ship and crew. But he still lacked one very important thing. He had no real friend.

Walton especially felt this absence because of his weak education. He had read little during his life except for poetry and sea books. A sympathetic but critical friend could have taught him many things.

But Walton knew perfectly well that he would find no such friend on this voyage. There were good men on the ship, though. He praised the qualities of his lieutenant, a bold and courageous Englishman. He was also pleased with the ship's master,[8] who—like Walton—didn't believe in treating sailors harshly.

Walton found both the lieutenant and the master very admirable. But neither of them had much education. Walton continued to feel the lack of a close friend.

Walton was determined to make his journey, though. For the time being, he was delayed in Archangel because of cold weather. But a warm spring was coming and might actually arrive sooner than expected. If so, Walton and his crew hoped to set sail before long.

Walton felt a mixture of fear and excitement about his coming journey. He was reminded of the story "The Rime of the Ancient Mariner."[9] That magical poem was one of the works that first inspired him to go to sea. But he assured his sister that—unlike the Ancient Mariner—he would kill no albatross.

Walton wondered when or if he would ever see his sister again. He asked her to write to him as much as possible and to remember him should he never return.

---

[8] A ship's master is second in command after the captain.
[9] "The Rime of the Ancient Mariner" is a long poem by Samuel Taylor Coleridge (1772-1834). The mariner (sailor) of the title kills an albatross, a harmless and innocent bird. His punishment for this cruel act is to tell his story again and again to anyone who will listen.

Letter 3 (Summary)

On July 7, Walton wrote to his sister from his ship. The letter was to be carried by a trading ship bound from Archangel to England.

Walton had little news to share, except for some stiff winds and a minor leak in the boat. The voyage had been going smoothly, and Walton was now on his way north. Sheets of floating ice surrounded the ship. But a warm summer wind blew out of the south. The sailors' spirits were excellent.

Walton promised to take no unnecessary risks on his journey. But he was almost boastful in his expectations of success. Walton ended his letter with blessings to his sister.

Letter 4

Vocabulary Preview

The following words appear in this letter. Review the list and get to know the words before you read the letter.

amiable—friendly; good-natured
existence—life
fatigue—extreme weariness or tiredness; exhaustion
harrowing—frightening; terrifying
moral—lesson; teaching
noble—impressive; of good character
perceived—noticed; became aware of
tormented—disturbed; upset

To Mrs. Saville, England

August 5th, 17—

Such a strange accident has happened to us that I can't help but to record it. However, it's very probable that you'll see me before you get these papers.

Last Monday (July 31st) we were nearly surrounded by ice. It closed in the ship on all sides. We barely had any sea-room in which to float.

Our situation was somewhat dangerous, especially since we were surrounded by a very thick fog. So we lay to[10] and hoped for a change in the weather.

About two o'clock the mist cleared away. We noticed huge, jagged plains of ice stretched out in every direction.

---

[10]*Lay to* means "to keep a ship motionless on the water."

They seemed to have no end. Some of my companions groaned. My own mind was filled with worried thoughts. Then a strange sight suddenly attracted our attention and made us forget our own situation.

We **perceived** a low carriage, fixed on a sledge and drawn by dogs. It was passing on towards the north at the distance of half a mile. A being which had the shape of a man—but apparently gigantic in size—sat in the sledge and guided the dogs.

We watched the quick progress of the traveler with our telescopes. At last he was lost among the distant stretches of the ice.

This appearance awakened our extreme wonder. We believed we were many hundred miles from any land. But this strange figure seemed to suggest otherwise. Perhaps land was not so far off as we had thought.

But we were shut in by the ice. That made it impossible to follow his track, which we had watched with the greatest attention.

About two hours after this occurrence, we heard the ground sea.[11] Before night the ice broke, and our ship was freed. However, we lay to until the morning. We feared hitting those large loose masses which float about after the breaking up of the ice. I took advantage of this time to rest for a few hours.

In the morning I went upon the deck as soon as it was light. I found all the sailors busy on one side of the ship. They seemed to be talking to someone in the sea. In fact, it was a sledge, like that we had seen before. This one had drifted toward us in the night on a large fragment of ice.

Only one dog remained alive. But there was also a human being in the sledge. And the sailors were trying to get him to board the ship. He was not—as the other traveler seemed to be—a savage being of some unknown land. Rather, he was a European.

When I appeared on the deck, the master said, "Here

---

[11]*Ground sea* is the same as a *ground swell*—a swell or movement in the ocean. In this case, the movement was strong enough to break up the ice.

is our captain. He will not allow you to perish on the open sea."

On seeing me, the stranger spoke in English, although with a foreign accent. "Before I come on board your ship," said he, "will you have the kindness to tell me where you are bound?"

You may imagine my surprise on hearing such a question. For it was addressed to me by a man on the edge of death. I should have thought that my ship would have been his rescuer—one he wouldn't have exchanged for the most precious wealth in the world.

However, I replied that we were on a voyage of discovery toward the northern pole. Upon hearing this he appeared satisfied and agreed to come on board. Thus he surrendered for his safety.

Good God! Margaret, if you had seen the man, your surprise would have been endless. His arms and legs were nearly frozen. His body was dreadfully thin from **fatigue** and suffering. I never saw a man in so miserable a condition. We tried to carry him into the cabin. But he fainted as soon as he had left the fresh air.

We accordingly brought him back to the deck and restored him to life by rubbing him with brandy. We forced him to swallow a small bit of it.

As soon as he showed signs of life we wrapped him up in blankets. Then we placed him near the chimney of the kitchen stove. Gradually, he recovered and ate a little soup. This restored him wonderfully.

Two days passed in this manner before he was able to speak. I often feared that his sufferings had affected his mind. But eventually he had somewhat recovered. I moved him to my own cabin and cared for him as much as my duty would permit.

I never saw a more interesting creature. His eyes generally have an expression of wildness, even madness. But—sometimes—when anyone is kind to him or does him the smallest service—his whole face lights up. He shines with a beam of kindness and sweetness that I never saw equaled.

But he is generally sad and despairing. Sometimes he grinds his teeth, as if impatient of the weight of misery that burdens him.

When my guest was a little recovered I had a hard time keeping off the men. They wished to ask him a thousand questions. But I wouldn't allow him to be **tormented** by their pointless curiosity. He needed complete rest in order to recover. Once, however, the lieutenant asked why he had come so far upon the ice in so strange a vehicle.

His face instantly took on a look of the deepest gloom. He replied, "To seek one who fled from me."

"And did the man whom you followed travel in the same way?"

"Yes."

"Then I believe we've seen him. The day before we picked you up we saw some dogs drawing a sledge across the ice. There was a man in it."

This aroused the stranger's attention. He asked an endless stream of questions. He wanted to know which way the demon, as he called him, had gone.

Soon afterwards he was alone with me. He said, "I have no doubt excited your curiosity, as well as that of these good people. But you're too kind to ask questions."

"Certainly. It would be very rude and inhuman of me to trouble you with my curiosity."

"And yet you rescued me from a strange and dangerous situation. You have kindly restored me to life."

Soon after this, he asked if I thought that the breaking up of the ice had destroyed the other sledge. I replied that I couldn't answer for certain. The ice hadn't broken until near midnight. The traveler might have arrived at a place of safety before that time. But I couldn't say for sure.

From this time, a new spirit of life strengthened the stranger's decaying body. He became eager to go on deck and watch for the sledge which had appeared before.

But I have persuaded him to remain in the cabin. He is far too weak to survive the raw atmosphere. I have promised that someone should watch for him. I will let him know the instant any new object should appear in sight.

Such is my journal relating to this strange occurrence up till now. The stranger has gradually improved in health. But he is very silent. And he appears uneasy when anyone except myself enters his cabin.

Yet his manners are charming and gentle. The sailors are all interested in him, although they've hardly spoken with him.

For my own part, I begin to love him as a brother. His constant and deep grief fills me with sympathy and concern. He must have been a **noble** creature in his better days. Even as a wreck he is attractive and **amiable.**

My dear Margaret, I said in one of my letters that I should find no friend on the wide ocean. Yet I have found a man who—before his spirit had been broken by misery—I should have been happy to have called the brother of my heart.

I shall continue my journal concerning the stranger from time to time, should I have any fresh incidents to tell about.

August 13th, 17—

My affection for my guest increases every day. He greatly excites both my admiration and my pity.

How can I see such a noble creature destroyed by misery without feeling the deepest grief? He is so gentle, yet so wise. His mind is extremely learned. When he speaks, his words are chosen carefully. But they flow quickly and with unequaled beauty.

He is now much recovered from his illness and is always on the deck. He's apparently watching for the sledge that went before his own. Yet, although unhappy, he's not completely caught up in his own misery. He is deeply interested in the concerns of others.

He has frequently spoken with me of mine, which I have shared with him in full. He listened closely to all my arguments that were in favor of my future success. Then he listened to every small detail of what I've done to ensure that success.

In the face of his deep sympathy, I spoke from the heart. I told of my soul's burning passion. I spoke of all the excitement that warmed me.

I told him I would gladly sacrifice my fortune, my **existence,** my every hope, to aid my task. One man's life or death was but a small price to pay to acquire the knowledge which I sought. I hoped to somehow find ways to control some of the enemies of nature.

As I spoke, a dark gloom spread over my listener's face. At first I saw that he tried to hide his emotion. He placed his hands over his eyes. My voice quivered and failed me as I watched him. Tears trickled fast from between his fingers. A groan burst from his heaving breast.

I paused. At last he spoke, in broken words: "Unhappy man! Do you share my madness? Have you also drunk the intoxicating potion? Hear me. Let me tell my tale, and you will dash the cup from your lips!"

As you may imagine, such words strongly aroused my curiosity. But the wild grief that had seized the stranger overcame his weakened powers. Many hours of rest and quiet talk were necessary to calm him.

At last he conquered the violence of his feelings. Then he appeared to hate himself for being the slave of passion. Quieting the dark cruelty of despair, he led me again to speak of myself.

He asked me the history of my earlier years. The tale was quickly told. But it awakened different memories within me.

I spoke of my desire to find a friend. I told him of my thirst for a closer friend than I have ever had. I told of my belief that a man without a true friend couldn't really be happy.

"I agree with you," replied the stranger. "Such a friend ought to be wiser, better, dearer than ourselves. Without him to help us better our faulty natures, we are incomplete creatures. We are only half made up.

"I once had a friend," he continued, "the most noble of human creatures. Therefore, I am qualified to judge about friendship. You have hope and the world before you. You have no cause for despair. But I—I have lost everything and can't begin my life over again."

As he said this his face expressed a calm, settled grief. It touched me to the heart. But he was silent and soon went to his cabin.

He is broken in spirit, Margaret. But even so, no one can feel the beauties of nature more deeply than he does. The starry sky, the sea, and every sight offered by these wonderful regions still seem to have the power of raising his soul.

Such a man has a double life. He may suffer misery and be overwhelmed by disappointments. Yet inside he is like a heavenly spirit surrounded by a halo. Within that halo, no grief or foolishness dares to go.

Will you smile at my enthusiasm concerning this divine wanderer? You wouldn't if you saw him. You have been taught and cultured by books. You live apart from the world. You are therefore somewhat hard to please.

But that only makes you more fit to appreciate the extraordinary qualities of this wonderful man. Sometimes I have tried to discover just what it is about him. What raises him so far above any other person I ever knew?

I believe it to be natural awareness, a quick but never-failing power of judgment. His clear, sharp understanding of things is unequaled. Add to this a sureness of expression and a voice whose tones are soul-quieting music.

August 19, 17—

Yesterday the stranger said to me, "You may easily see, Captain Walton, that I have suffered great misfortunes. At one time I was determined to forget all about these evils. But you have made me change my mind.

"You seek for knowledge and wisdom, as I once did," he went on. "I strongly hope that the satisfaction of your wishes may not be a serpent to sting you, as mine has been.

"I don't know if the story of my disasters will be useful to you. Yet I can see that you are following the same course. You are exposing yourself to the same dangers which have made me what I am. So I imagine that you may find a correct **moral** in my tale. It may guide you if you succeed in your undertaking. Yet it will also comfort you in case of failure.

"Prepare to hear of events which are usually thought of as impossible. If we were among the tamer scenes of nature, I would fear to face your unbelief, perhaps your ridicule.

"But many things will appear possible in these wild and mysterious regions. You may not feel the urge to laugh like those who live normal lives. Nor can I doubt but that my tale proves itself true. As the story unfolds, you will see its own evidence of the truth."

Margaret, you may easily imagine the pleasure I felt at this offer. Yet I couldn't bear that he should renew his grief by speaking of his misfortunes.

Still, I felt the greatest eagerness to hear the promised tale. Part of it was curiosity. Part of it was a strong desire to help him if I could. I told him this.

"I thank you for your sympathy," he replied. "But it is useless. My fate is nearly fulfilled. I wait only for one event, and then I shall rest in peace.

"I understand your feeling," he continued, seeing that I wished to interrupt him. "But if you will allow me to say so, my friend, you are mistaken. Nothing can change my fate. Listen to my history, and you will see how completely it is decided."

He then told me that he would begin his tale the next

day. I thanked him warmly.

He will tell his story to me in his own words during the day. I will record it every night when I am able. If I should be occupied, I will at least make notes.

This manuscript will doubtless give you the greatest pleasure. His tale is different to me, who know him and who hear it from his own lips. With what interest and sympathy shall I read it in some future day!

Even now, as I begin my task, his full-toned voice swells in my ears. His sparkling eyes dwell on me with all their sad sweetness. I see his thin hand raised in movement. The features of his face are lighted by the soul within.

Strange and **harrowing** must be his story. And frightful must be the storm which surrounded the brave ship on its course and wrecked it—thus!

Chapter 1

Vocabulary Preview

The following words appear in this chapter. Review the list and get to know the words before you read the chapter.

abode—home; dwelling
exotic—unusual; different
prosperity—wealth
tranquillity—peacefulness; calmness

I am a Genevese by birth. My family is one of the most respected of that republic.[1] For many years my ancestors held high offices there. And my father, Alphonse Frankenstein, had filled several public offices with honor. He was respected by all those who knew him. People admired his honesty and unending attention to public business.

My father spent his younger days busy with the affairs of his country. Several different circumstances had prevented his marrying early. It wasn't until middle age that he became a husband and the father of a family.

The circumstances of his marriage tell much about his character. So I must tell about them. One of his closest friends was a merchant who had suffered many misfortunes. Because of his bad luck, this merchant fell from **prosperity** into poverty.

This man—whose name was Beaufort—was stubborn and proud. He couldn't bear to live forgotten and in poverty. He also didn't like the thought of staying in the

---

[1] In 1535, the city of Geneva, Switzerland, adopted the Protestant religion and became an independent city-state.

same country where he was once respected and admired.
So he paid his debts in the most honorable manner.
Then he moved with his daughter to the town of Lucerne.
There he lived unknown and broken-hearted.

My father loved Beaufort with the truest friendship.
He was deeply upset by his friend's unfortunate
circumstances. He also disliked his friend's false pride. He
saw Beaufort's behavior as little worthy of the affection
that held the two of them together.

So my father lost no time seeking Beaufort out. He
hoped to persuade him to begin the world again through
his credit and help.

Beaufort had taken strong measures to hide himself.
So it was ten months before my father discovered his
abode. It turned out that Beaufort lived on a poor street
near the Reuss. Overjoyed at this discovery, my father
hurried to the house. But when he entered, only misery
and despair welcomed him.

Beaufort had saved only a very small sum of money
from his fortunes. But it was enough to provide him with
food for some months. In the meantime, Beaufort hoped
to find a respectable job in a merchant's house. While he
waited, he was able to do nothing. And his grief only
became more deep and bitter. At last it took fast hold of
his mind. After three months he was quite ill, unable to
do much of anything.

His daughter cared for him with the greatest
tenderness. But she saw with despair that their little fund
was quickly running out. There was no other means of
support.

But Caroline Beaufort possessed an unusual mind.
Her courage supported her, and she found plain work.
She wove straw, and in one way or another, managed to
earn a tiny wage. But it was hardly enough to support two
people.

Several months passed in this way. Caroline's father
grew worse. Her time was almost entirely spent in caring
for him. Her means of living grew smaller. In the tenth

month her father died in her arms, leaving her an orphan and a beggar.

This last blow overwhelmed her. She knelt by Beaufort's coffin and was weeping bitterly when my father entered the room. He came like a protecting spirit to the poor girl, who turned herself over to his care.

After the burial of his friend, my father took her to Geneva. There he placed her under the care of relatives. Two years after this event, Caroline became his wife.

There was quite a difference between the ages of my parents. But this seemed only to draw them closer in bonds of devoted affection. There was a strong sense of justice in my father's upright mind. He could only love a person whom he approved of. Perhaps he had once suffered by discovering that someone he had loved had let him down. So he tended to set a greater value on true worth.

There was a show of great worship in his attachment to my mother. It was completely different from the adoring fondness of age. It was inspired by respect for her goodness. He also desired somewhat to make up for the sorrows she had endured.

All this gave tremendous grace to his behavior to her. Everything was done according to her wishes and her convenience. He tried to shelter her like a gardener shelters a rare and **exotic** plant. He protected her from every rough wind. He surrounded her with all that would make her happy.

Her health had been shaken by what she had gone through. So had the **tranquillity** of her once-determined spirit.

During the two years before their marriage, my father had gradually given up all his public duties. Immediately after their union they sought the pleasant climate of Italy. This tour through that land of wonders was a needed change of scene and interest. It helped restore her weakened frame.

From Italy they visited Germany and France. I, their

eldest child, was born at Naples. As an infant, I went with them on their journeys. For several years I remained their only child. Much as they were attached to each other, they also heaped endless affection on me. It was as if they drew all their feelings from a well of love.

My mother's tender touches and my father's smile of pleasure are my first memories. I was their plaything and their idol. And I was also something better. I was their child, the innocent and helpless creature given to them by heaven.

I was theirs to bring up to be a good person. My future happiness or misery was in their hands. All this depended on how they carried out their duties towards me.

They were deeply aware of what they owed their offspring. They were also moved by an active spirit of tenderness. So I constantly received lessons of patience, of charity, and of self-control. I was guided in a most enjoyable way.

For a long time I was their only care. My mother much desired to have a daughter, but I continued as their single offspring.

When I was about five years old, my parents made a trip beyond the frontiers of Italy. They spent a week on the shores of the Lake of Como.[2]

Their kindly nature often led them to visit the cottages of the poor. To my mother, this was more than a duty. It was a necessity, a passion for her to act as the guardian angel to the unlucky. She remembered what she herself had suffered and how she had been relieved.

During one of their walks, a poor cottage in the bottom of a valley attracted their notice. A number of half-clothed children who gathered about it spoke of poverty at its worst.

One day, my mother visited this house, and I went with her. It was a day my father had gone by himself to

---

[2] The Lake of Como is the third largest lake in Italy.

Milan.[3] Arriving at the cottage, my mother found a hard-working peasant and his wife. They seemed bent down from care and labor. They were passing around a skimpy meal to five hungry babes. Among these children was one which my mother noticed far above all the rest. This girl appeared to be different from all the others. They were dark-eyed, hardy little rascals. But this child was thin and very fair. Her hair was the brightest living gold. And despite her ragged clothing, she somehow seemed noble.

Her forehead was clear and good-sized and her blue eyes cloudless. Her lips and the shape of her face told of intelligence and sweetness. No one could look at her without seeing she was different. She bore the stamp of heaven in all her features.

The peasant woman noticed that my mother looked with wonder and admiration on this lovely girl. She eagerly told her all about the child.

The girl wasn't hers, but the daughter of a nobleman of Milan. Her mother was a German and had died at the child's birth. The infant had been placed with these good people. They had been better off back then. They hadn't been long married, and their eldest child was but just born.

The girl's father was one of those Italians linked with the memory of the old glory of Italy. He was one among the *schiavi ognor frementi*,[4] who struggled to obtain the freedom of his country.

He became a victim of its weakness. Whether he had died or still remained in the dungeons of Austria wasn't known. His property was seized. His child became an orphan and a beggar. She continued with her foster parents and bloomed in their rough home. She was fairer than a garden rose among dark-leaved shrubs.

When my father returned from Milan, he found a

---

[3] Milan is a city in northern Italy.
[4] "Slaves continually trembling." This phrase refers to those who rebelled against Austrian rule.

child fairer than a pictured cherub[5] playing with me in the hall of our house. Her looks shone. Her form and motions were lighter than the chamois[6] of the hills.

The girl was soon explained. With his permission, my mother persuaded the girl's poor guardians to give their adopted child to her. The couple were fond of the sweet orphan. Her presence had seemed a blessing to them. But it would be unfair to her to keep her in poverty and want when Providence[7] offered her such powerful protection.

The peasant couple spoke with their village priest. The result was that Elizabeth Lavenza came to live with us. She was my more than sister. She was the beautiful and adored companion of all my occupations and my pleasures.

Everyone loved Elizabeth. They regarded her with a passionate and almost holy love. The feeling Elizabeth stirred in others became my pride and my delight. Not that I didn't also share the feeling.

On the evening before she was brought to my home, my mother had said playfully, "I have a pretty present for my Victor. Tomorrow he shall have it."

And then the next day she presented Elizabeth to me as her promised gift. With childish seriousness, I took her words to heart and looked upon Elizabeth as mine. She was mine to protect, love, and cherish. All praises heaped on her became praises for one of my own possessions.

We called each other by the name of cousin. No word, no expression could describe the kind of relationship I felt I had with her. She was more than my sister, since till death she was to be mine only.

---

[5] A cherub is a high-ranking angel, often shown as a sweet-faced child.
[6] A chamois is a goat-sized antelope.
[7] Providence is the kindly guidance of God.

Chapter 2 (Summary)

Victor continued to tell of his and Elizabeth's childhood. There was not quite a year's difference between their ages. Elizabeth was poetic and artistic. Victor was more interested in science. From an early age, he took great delight in exploring nature.

When Victor was seven years old, his first brother was born. At this time, his parents settled in Geneva for good. Victor attended school there. But he spent little time with his schoolmates, with one exception. This was a merchant's son named Henry Clerval. Henry was a child with a huge imagination. He had a talent for writing poetry and plays.

Victor remembered his childhood as very happy. True, he had a hot temper at times. But his true passion was his interest in science. Indeed, he found no other subject very interesting. He became more and more curious about the secrets of the universe.

Clerval's interests dealt more with people. He hoped to grow up to help humankind. In the meantime, Elizabeth exercised a warm and loving influence on the two boys.

Victor's childhood offered little hint of the misery to come. But he could now trace how disaster and tragedy were to come about.

Among the sciences, Victor especially liked natural philosophy.[1] This field caught his fancy when he was thirteen and came across a copy of a book by Cornelius Agrippa.[2] Agrippa's theories fascinated him.

Victor told his father about his interest in Agrippa. But his father told him not to waste his time on such "sad trash." Looking back, Victor wished his father had explained that Agrippa's ideas were outdated. If he had,

---

[1] Natural philosophy is now generally described as science.
[2] Cornelius Agrippa (1486-1535) was a German philosopher. In his time, science and magic were not yet clearly separated.

Victor might have been drawn away from future unhappiness.

Victor read more and more of Agrippa. He also read works by Paracelsus and Albertus Magnus.[3] He felt a burning desire to follow in their footsteps. In particular, he wanted to find what they had sought—the secret of life. Victor hoped someday to rid humankind of disease and even death. He had no way to know that the ancient alchemists were closer to magic than science. He knew nothing of more recent discoveries.

When he was fifteen, Victor saw a mighty oak tree blasted to a stump by lightning. This was his first encounter with electricity, a powerful force which made his favorite authors seem unimportant. For a while afterwards, Victor lost his interest in the deeper secrets of nature. He spent his time on more practical studies.

Victor now looked back on this as the effort of a kindly guardian spirit to save him. But fate had already decided the direction his life would take. He was doomed to an evil end.

---

[3] Paracelsus (1493-1541) was a Swiss alchemist. An alchemist was someone who tried to change common metals into gold by magical and scientific means. Albertus Magnus (c. 1200-1280) was a German scientist and religious thinker, often thought of as a magician.

Chapter 3

When I was seventeen, my parents decided that I should attend the University of Ingolstadt.[1] Before then I had attended the schools of Geneva. But my father thought I should be aware of other customs than those of my native country. He considered it a necessary part of a complete education.

My departure was therefore fixed at an early date. But before the day arrived, the first misfortune of my life occurred. It was an **omen,** as it were, of my future misery.

Elizabeth had caught the scarlet fever.[2] Her illness was severe, and she was in the greatest danger.

During her illness we tried hard to persuade my mother to keep far away from her. She had at first given in to our wishes. But soon she heard that the life of her favorite was threatened. Then my mother could no longer

---

[1] Between 1472 and 1800, the German city of Ingolstadt was known for its fine university.
[2] Scarlet fever is a disease which causes a red rash and high fever.

control her worry. She began caring for Elizabeth herself. Her loving attention helped gain victory over the evil disease.

Elizabeth was saved. But my mother's risk was fatal to her. After three days my mother became ill. Her fever was accompanied by the most alarming symptoms. We feared the worst for her.

On her deathbed, the courage and kindness of this best of women didn't leave her. She joined the hands of Elizabeth and myself.

"My children," she said, "my firmest hopes of future happiness were placed on your marriage one day. This hope will now be a comfort to your father.

"Elizabeth, my love, you must take my place with the younger children. Alas! I regret that I am taken from you. Happy and beloved as I have been, is it not hard to leave you all?

"But these aren't suitable thoughts for me. I will try to resign myself cheerfully to death. And I won't let go of my hope of meeting you in another world."

My mother died calmly, and her face expressed love even in death. I don't need to describe the feelings of those who experience the death of a loved one. An emptiness presents itself to the soul, and despair is shown on the face. It is long before the mind realizes the truth.

The mind tries to accept the loss of one whom we saw every day. Her very being appeared a part of our own, and now she has gone forever. The brightness of a beloved eye has been put out. The sound of a voice so familiar and dear to the ear has been hushed. It will never again be heard.

These are the thoughts of the first days. Eventually, with the passing of time, the actual bitterness of grief begins.

Yet is there anyone from whom a loved one hasn't been torn away? And why should I describe a sorrow which all have felt, and must feel?

The time at last arrives when grief is no longer

necessary. The smile that plays upon the lips may be thought disrespectful. Still, it doesn't go away.

My mother was dead, but we still had duties which we had to perform. We needed to go on with our lives. We had to learn to think ourselves fortunate as long as we were all alive.

My departure for Ingolstadt had been delayed by these events. It was now planned again, though I persuaded my father to put it off a few more weeks. It seemed wrong to me to leave the calmness of the house of mourning so soon. The calmness was much like death. It was hard to rush into the thick of life.

I was new to sorrow. But it didn't alarm me any less. I didn't want to leave those that remained to me. Above all, I wished to see my sweet Elizabeth comforted more.

She indeed hid her grief and tried to comfort us all. She took on life's duties with courage and spirit. The dear girl devoted herself to those whom she called her uncle and cousins.

Elizabeth was never so enchanting as she was at this time. She brought back the sunshine of her smiles and spent them upon us. She forgot even her own regret in her attempts to make us forget.

The day of my departure finally arrived. Clerval spent the last evening with us. He had tried to persuade his father to let him go with me and become my fellow student. But his tries were in vain. His father was a narrow-minded trader. And he saw no point in his son's hopes and ambitions.

Henry felt he was being held back from a full education. In his misfortune, he said little. But when he spoke I read a quiet but firm determination in his sharp eye and in his lively glance. He wouldn't be chained to the miserable details of business.

We sat late. We couldn't tear ourselves away from each other. Nor could we persuade ourselves to say the word "Farewell!" It was said at last, and we separated with the excuse of seeking rest. Each of us fancied that the other was fooled. But at morning's dawn, when I went down to the carriage, they were all there.

My father was there to bless me, and Clerval to press my hand once more. And my Elizabeth kept asking me to write often. She **bestowed** her final attentions on her playmate and friend.

I threw myself into the carriage that was to carry me away. There I dwelled on the saddest thoughts. I had always been surrounded by friends. I was always taking pleasure in their company.

But now I was alone. In the university where I was going, I must make new friends and look out for myself.

Until then, my life had been remarkably sheltered. Because of this, I had a great dislike of new faces. I loved my brothers, and Elizabeth, and Clerval. These were "old familiar faces." But I believed I was totally unprepared for the company of strangers.

Such were my thoughts as I began my journey. But as I continued, my spirits and hopes rose.

I eagerly desired to gain knowledge. When at home, I had often thought it hard to remain cooped up in one place during my youth. I had longed to enter the world and take my place among other human beings. Now my desires were fulfilled. Indeed, it would have been foolish to feel sorry.

I had plenty of time for these and many other thoughts during my journey to Ingolstadt. The trip was long and tiring. At length, the high white steeple[3] of the town met my eyes. I stepped out and was led to my solitary apartment to spend the evening as I pleased.

The next morning I delivered my letters of introduction. I also paid a visit to some of the professors.

I must say that chance had taken a complete hold on me from the moment I turned my reluctant steps from my father's door. Or rather, it was the evil influence—the Angel of Destruction.

---

[3] A steeple is a church tower.

It was chance that led me first to M. Krempe,[4] professor of natural philosophy. He was an ill-mannered man. But he was deeply learned in the secrets of his science. He asked me several questions. Most concerned my progress in the different branches of science relating to natural philosophy.

I replied carelessly. Partly in **contempt,** I mentioned the names of my alchemists as the main authors I had studied. The professor stared.

"Have you," he said, "really spent your time in studying such nonsense?"

I replied that I had.

"Every minute," continued M. Krempe with anger, "every instant that you have wasted on those books is completely lost. You have burdened your memory with outdated theories and useless names.

"Good God!" the professor went on. "In what desert land have you lived? Did no one inform you that these ideas are a thousand years old? They are as musty as they are ancient!

"To find a follower of Albertus Magnus and Paracelsus!" said Professor Krempe. "I hardly expected such a thing in this enlightened and scientific age. My dear sir, you must begin your studies all over again."

So saying, he stepped aside. He wrote down a list of several books on natural philosophy which he desired me to find.

He mentioned that he intended to begin a course of lectures on the topic of natural philosophy. He would start them at the beginning of the following week. He added that M. Waldman—a fellow professor—would also offer a series of lectures upon chemistry. Then he dismissed me.

I returned home not disappointed. I have said that I had long felt those authors whom the professor criticized were useless. But I wasn't about to become a follower of

---

[4] *M.* is an abbreviation for "Monsieur," which is French for "Mister."

M. Krempe either.

M. Krempe was a little squat man with a gruff voice and an ugly face. And I didn't look upon his studies with any more favor. I have just told you of the conclusions I had reached about such studies in my early years. Perhaps I have done so in rather a too logical way.

As a child, I hadn't been satisfied with the results promised by the modern professors of natural science. I can only explain that my confusion of ideas came about because I was young. I also lacked a guide in such matters.

I had followed the steps of knowledge backwards through time. I had then exchanged the discoveries of recent scientists for the dreams of forgotten alchemists.

Besides, I had a contempt for the uses of modern natural philosophy. It had been very different when the masters of the science sought power and the ability to live forever. Those views were grand, although useless. My interest in science was mainly founded on such visions.

But now the scene was changed. The aim of the scientist seemed to be to destroy those visions. I was expected to exchange visions of boundless greatness for realities that were worth little.

Such were my thoughts during the first two or three days of my stay at Ingolstadt. These days were mainly spent in becoming acquainted with the local places and the residents in my new home.

Then the next week came. I thought of the information which M. Krempe had given me about the lectures. I refused to go and hear that little **conceited** fellow speak. But I remembered what he had said of M. Waldman. I had never seen him, as he had been out of town until then.

Partly from curiosity and partly because I had nothing else to do, I went into the lecture room. M. Waldman entered shortly after.

This professor was very unlike M. Krempe. He

appeared about fifty years of age. His face showed great kindness. A few gray hairs covered his temples, but those at the back of his head were nearly black. He was short, but he stood remarkably straight. His voice was the sweetest I had ever heard.

The professor began his lecture by retelling the history of chemistry. He described the various improvements made by different men of learning. He spoke with feeling the names of the most respected discoverers. He also gave a brief view of the present state of science and explained many of its basic terms.

He then performed a few experiments. At last, he finished the lecture with enthusiastic praise to modern chemistry. I shall never forget his words:

"The ancient teachers of this science," said he, "promised impossibilities and performed nothing. The modern masters promise very little. They know that metals cannot be changed and that the elixir of life[5] is a fantasy.

"The hands of these modern men seem made only to dabble in dirt. Their eyes might have been made just to pore over the microscope or crucible.[6] But they have indeed performed miracles.

"They dig into the depths of nature and show how she works in her hiding places. They rise into the heavens. They have discovered how the blood circulates, and what is in the air we breathe.

"They have acquired new and almost unlimited powers. They can command the thunders of the heaven, mimic the earthquake, and even mock the invisible world with its own shadows."

Such were the professor's words—or rather let me say the words of fate. They were spoken to destroy me. As he went on, I felt as if my soul were struggling with a physical enemy. One by one, the various keys were

---

[5] The elixir of life was a potion sought by alchemists. Its purpose was to allow people to live forever.
[6] A crucible was a scientist's container for melting gold.

touched which formed the workings of my being. Chord after chord was sounded.

Soon my mind was filled with one thought, one idea, one purpose. "So much has been done," exclaimed the soul of Victor Frankenstein. "More, far more, will I achieve. Following the steps already marked, I'll pioneer a new way. I will explore the unknown powers. And I'll unfold to the world the deepest mysteries of creation."

I didn't close my eyes that night. My mind was in a state of struggle and confusion. I felt that order would arise sometime, but I had no power to produce it.

After the morning's dawn, sleep came gradually. I awoke, and the thoughts of the night before were like a dream. All that remained was a decision to return to my old studies. I decided to devote myself to a science in which I believed I had a natural talent.

On the same day, I paid M. Waldman a visit. His manners in private were even more mild and attractive than in public. There had been a certain dignity in his expression during his lecture. In his own house this expression was replaced by the greatest friendliness and kindness.

I told him pretty nearly the same story of my past studies as I had given to his fellow professor. He listened with attention to this little tale. He smiled at the names of Cornelius Agrippa and Paracelsus. But he didn't show the contempt that M. Krempe had displayed.

"These men had endless enthusiasm," he said. "Modern scientists owe them a great deal for most of their knowledge. They left us an easier task.

"We can give new names to things," the professor said. "We can arrange our facts in related groups. In a great degree, these men were the instruments that helped bring these possibilities to light. The labors of geniuses may be turned in the wrong direction. But they almost always turn finally to the advantage of mankind."

I listened to this statement, which was delivered without any boldness or pretense. Then I added that his lecture had removed my **prejudices** against modern chemists. I spoke carefully. I showed the modesty and respect due from a youth to his instructor.

I didn't show any enthusiasm for the work I intended to do. Inexperience in life would have made me ashamed to do so. Instead, I requested his advice on the books I ought to get.

"I'm happy to have gained a follower," said M. Waldman. "And if your discipline equals your ability, I have no doubt of your success.

"Chemistry is the branch of science in which the greatest improvements have been and may be made. It is for that reason that I have made it my own study.

"But at the same time, I haven't forgotten about the other branches of science. A man would make a very poor chemist if he only thought about chemistry.

"I take it that your wish is to truly become a man of science. You don't wish to be just a small-time experimentalist. I should advise you to study every branch of natural philosophy. This includes mathematics."

He then took me into his laboratory and explained to me the uses of his various machines. He told me what instruments I ought to obtain. Then he promised me the use of his own instruments. But first I had to advance far enough in the science not to damage them. After he gave me a list of the books which I had requested, I left.

Thus ended a memorable day. It decided my future fate.

Chapter 4

Vocabulary Preview

The following words appear in this chapter. Review the list and get to know the words before you read the chapter.

pursuit—search; purpose
repulsive—disgusting; unpleasant
sensations—feelings related to the senses
    (taste, touch, smell, sound, sight)
theory—idea; concept
toil—work; labor

From this day, science became almost my only occupation. I was particularly interested in chemistry. I eagerly read the works which modern scientists have written on these subjects. I found them full of genius and good judgment.

I attended the lectures and got to know the men of science of the university. I even found a great deal of sound sense and real information in M. Krempe. It's true they were combined with a **repulsive** appearance and manners. But he wasn't any less valuable because of that.

In M. Waldman I found a true friend. His gentleness was never stained by narrow-mindedness. His instructions were clear and given good-naturedly. And his actions gave no hint of pride.

In a thousand ways M. Waldman smoothed the path of knowledge for me. He made the most difficult ideas clear and easy to my mind. I was shaky and uncertain when I first began my studies. But I gained strength as time went on, and I soon became an eager student. The stars often disappeared in the morning light while I was still busy in my laboratory.

I worked very hard. So it may be easily imagined that I advanced quickly. Indeed, my fellow students wondered at my eagerness. And the professors were amazed at my skill. Professor Krempe often asked me with a sly smile how Cornelius Agrippa went on. At the same time, M. Waldman expressed the most heartfelt excitement in my progress.

Two years passed in this manner. During this time I paid no visit to Geneva. I was engaged heart and soul in the quest of some discoveries which I hoped to make.

Only those who have experienced the joy of discovery can imagine the lure of science. In other studies you go as far as others have gone before you. Then there is nothing more to know. But in science there is always food for discovery and wonder.

A mind of average abilities which studies one subject very closely must surely gain great skill in that study. So I stuck always to one object of **pursuit.** I was totally wrapped up in my work, and I improved very quickly.

At the end of two years I discovered how to improve some chemical instruments. Because of this, I gained great respect and admiration at the university.

At last, I had arrived at a point where I was very familiar with the **theory** and practice of natural philosophy. I could gain nothing more from the lessons of the professors at Ingolstadt. So my stay there was no longer helpful to my improvements.

I thought then of returning to my friends and my native town. But then something happened that made my stay longer.

One of the wonders which had particularly attracted my attention was the structure of the human body. Indeed, I was interested in any living animal. Where, I often asked myself, did the nature of life come from?

It was a bold question. And it was one which has

always been considered a mystery. Yet think of how many things we are on the edge of discovering. If only cowardice or carelessness didn't keep back our questions. I turned these thoughts over in my mind. I decided from then on to apply myself more particularly to physiology.[1] I was driven by an almost supernatural enthusiasm. Otherwise, my studies would have been unpleasant and almost unbearable.

To examine the causes of life, we must first have access to death. I became acquainted with the science of anatomy.[2] But this wasn't enough. I also had to observe the natural decay of the human body.

My father had carefully planned my education. He saw to it that my mind shouldn't be impressed with any supernatural horrors. I don't ever remember trembling at a tale of superstition. I never feared the vision of a ghost.

Darkness had no effect upon my imagination. To me, a churchyard was just a place for bodies of the dead. These bodies—after being the seat of beauty and strength—had merely become food for the worm.

Now I was led to examine the cause and progress of this decay. I was forced to spend days and nights in vaults and charnel-houses.[3] My attention was fixed on every object which was most offensive to human feelings.

I saw how the fine form of human bodies rotted. I beheld the decay of death on the blooming cheek of life. I saw how the wonders of the eye and brain belonged to the worm.

I paused, examining and analyzing all the tiniest causes of death. I studied anything that explained the change from life to death, and death to life. At last—from the midst of this darkness—a sudden light broke in upon me. It was a brilliant and wondrous light, yet simple too.

I became dizzy with the number of possibilities it showed. So many men of genius had studied the same

---

[1] Physiology is the study of living things.
[2] Anatomy is a science that deals with the structure of living things.
[3] Charnel-houses are places where the dead are placed in tombs.

science. I was surprised that—among them all—I alone should be allowed to discover such an astonishing secret.

Remember, I'm not recording the vision of a madman. The sun shines in the heavens as surely as what I'm about to say is true. Some miracle might have produced it. Yet the stages of discovery were clear and logical.

My days and nights were filled with labor and exhaustion. At last, I succeeded in discovering the cause of birth and life. What's more, I became myself capable of giving life to lifeless matter.

At first I experienced astonishment on this discovery. This feeling soon changed to delight and excitement. I had spent so much time in painful labor. To arrive at the peak of my desires was the most satisfying end to my struggles.

But this discovery was so great and overwhelming that all the steps that led to it were forgotten. I saw only the result. This had been the study and desire of the wisest men since the creation of the world. And now it was within my reach.

Not that it all opened up to me at once, like a magic scene. The information I had obtained was of a different nature than that. I would use this knowledge to direct me toward the object of my search. I saw no point in showing others what I had done so far. I was like the Arabian who had been buried and found a passage to life, aided only by one seemingly weak light.[4]

I see your eagerness and the wonder and hope which your eyes show, my friend. You expect me to inform you of my secret. That cannot be. Listen patiently until the end of my story. Then you will easily see why I feel the way I do.

You are as unguarded and eager as I was then. I won't lead you on to your ruin and certain misery. Learn from me how dangerous it is to gain knowledge. Learn how

---

[4] This refers to an episode in "The Fourth Voyage of Sindbad the Sailor" from *The Arabian Nights.*

happy that man is who believes his hometown is the world. That man is happier than he who wants to become greater than he was meant to be. At least learn by my example, if not by what I say.

I had found an astonishing power placed within my hands. But I hesitated a long time concerning how I should use it. True, I possessed the means of giving life. But a frame for receiving that life required complicated webs of fibers, muscles, and veins. This remained a work of great difficulty and labor.

I wondered at first whether I should try to create a being like myself or a simpler one. But my imagination was thrilled by my first success. It wouldn't allow me to doubt myself. I knew I had the ability to give life to an animal as wonderful as man.

The materials I had at the time hardly seemed enough for such a difficult task. But I didn't doubt that I should finally succeed.

I prepared myself for many setbacks. My experiments might fail again and again. And at the end my work might be imperfect.

Yet I considered the improvement which takes place every day in science. This encouraged me to hope my present tries would at least lay the way for future success. Nor could I consider the difficulty of my plan as any argument of its failure. It was with these feelings that I began to create a human being.

The smallness of the parts greatly slowed me down. So I changed my mind and decided to make the being of a gigantic size. It was to be about eight feet in height, and large all over. After I made this decision, I spent some months in collecting and arranging my materials. Then I began.

No one can imagine the feelings which carried me onwards in the first excitement of success. It was like a hurricane. The boundaries of life and death seemed purely imaginary. I needed first to break through the boundaries and pour a stream of light into our dark world.

A new species[5] would bless me as its creator and source of life. Many happy and excellent beings would owe their lives to me. No father could claim the love of his child more than I should deserve theirs.

With these ideas in mind, I thought of what it might mean if I could give life to lifeless matter. After some time, I might (although I now found it impossible) restore life where death had apparently claimed the body.

These thoughts kept my spirits up, while I went at my task with untiring energy. My cheek had grown pale with overwork. My body had become thin and weak from being shut inside. Sometimes I failed on the very edge of success.

Yet still I hung on to the hope which the next day or the next hour might realize. One secret which I alone possessed was the hope to which I had dedicated myself. The moon gazed on my midnight labors while I pursued nature to her hiding places. I worked on with tense and breathless eagerness.

Who shall imagine the horrors of my secret **toil?** I dabbled among the unholy damps of the grave. I tortured living animals while trying to make my experiment work. My body now trembles, and my eyes swim with the memory.

But at the time, a strong and almost wild feeling urged me on. I seemed to have lost all soul or feeling but for this one pursuit. Indeed, it was only a passing trance. I realized this only after my unnatural fascination passed. Then I felt normal **sensations** with more sharpness than before.

As it was, I collected bones from charnel-houses. With sinful fingers, I disturbed the great secrets of the human frame. I worked in a lonely chamber—or rather, cell—at the top of the house. It was separated from all the other apartments by a hallway and staircase. There I

---

[5] A species is a group of things having the same traits or features. For example, human beings belong to one species.

kept my workshop of filthy creation. My eyeballs burned from attending to the details of my work. The dissecting room[6] and the slaughter-house furnished many of my materials. Often I turned with disgust from my work. But still, my eagerness again increased, and I brought my work near to an end. The summer months passed while I was thus engaged, heart and soul, in my pursuit. It was the most beautiful season. Never did the fields yield a more plentiful harvest or the vines yield more abundant fruit. But my eyes were blind to the charms of nature. Not only did I neglect the scenes around me. I also forgot those friends who were so far away. I hadn't written them for a very long time. I knew my silence worried them. And I well remembered the words of my father: "I know that while you are pleased with yourself you'll think of us with affection. We shall then hear regularly from you. You must pardon me if I regard any lack of correspondence as proof that your other duties are also neglected."

Therefore, I knew well what my father's feelings would be. But I couldn't tear my thoughts from my labor. My work was distasteful in itself. But it had a hold on my imagination that wouldn't let loose.

As it were, I wished to put all of my feelings of affection on hold. I wanted to wait until my great object should be completed. In the meantime, my task swallowed up my whole being.

At that time, I thought that my father was unfair if he thought my neglect was all my fault. But I'm now convinced that he was justified in thinking that I shouldn't be completely free from blame.

A human being in perfection ought to always have a calm and peaceful mind. He should never allow passion or a passing desire to disturb his good judgment. I don't think that the pursuit of knowledge is an exception to this rule.

---

[6] Dissecting is separating animal parts for scientific study.

A study to which you apply yourself may tend to weaken your affections. It may destroy your taste for simpler pleasures. If so, that study is certainly unlawful. That is to say, it isn't fit for the human mind. This rule ought always to have been followed. Then no man would have allowed any quest at all to interfere with the calmness of his home life. If this had been so, Greece wouldn't have been enslaved, and Caesar would have spared his country. America would have been discovered more gradually, and the empires of Mexico and Peru wouldn't have been destroyed.[7]

But I forget that I am moralizing in the most interesting part of my tale. Your looks remind me to go on.

My father didn't scold me in his letters. He only took notice of my silence by asking about my studies more particularly than before.

Winter, spring, and summer passed away during my labors. I didn't watch the blossom or the growing leaves. These sights had before always given me supreme delight. But now I was too caught up in my work to notice them.

The leaves of that year had withered before my work drew near to a close. Now every day showed me more plainly how well I had succeeded. But worry held back my enthusiasm. I was rather like one doomed by slavery to work in the mines or some other unhealthful trade. I certainly didn't seem like an artist occupied by his favorite employment.

Every night I was worn down by a slow fever. I became nervous to a most painful degree. The fall of a leaf startled me, and I avoided my fellow creatures as if I had been guilty of a crime. Sometimes I grew alarmed at the wreck I believed

---

[7] During its "Golden Age" (460-429 B.C.), the Greek city-state of Athens was known for its culture and democracy. Afterwards, it became increasingly warlike. Julius Caesar (100-44 B.C.) was assassinated for having become too powerful in the Roman Empire. The colonization of America was terribly destructive to its native peoples. The Spanish conquered the Mexican Aztecs in 1521 and the Incas of Peru in 1532.

that I had become. The energy of my purpose alone kept me going. My labors would soon end. I believed that exercise and amusement would then drive away the beginning of disease. I promised myself both of these when my creation should be complete.

Chapter 5

It was on a dreary night of November that I looked at what I had done. I felt an anxiety that almost amounted to agony. I collected the instruments of life around me. Then I set about bringing a spark of being to the lifeless thing that lay at my feet.

It was already one in the morning. The rain pattered gloomily against the panes, and my candle was nearly burnt out. Then, by the glimmer of the half-extinguished light, I saw the dull yellow eye of the creature open. The being breathed hard. Its limbs shook violently.

How can I describe my emotions at this awful event? How can I describe the **wretch** whom I had formed with such care? I had made all his parts correctly, and I had selected his features as beautiful.

Beautiful! Great God! His yellow skin scarcely covered the muscles and arteries[1] beneath. True, his hair

---

[1] Arteries are vessels which carry blood away from the heart to other parts of the body.

was shiny black and flowing. And his teeth were pearly white. But these features only made a more horrid contrast with the rest of his face. His watery eyes seemed almost of the same color as the dull white sockets in which they were set. His skin was shriveled and his straight lips were black.

Nothing is so changeable as the feelings of human nature. I had worked hard for nearly two years. My one purpose had been to bring life to a lifeless body. For this I had deprived myself of rest and health. I had desired my goal with an eagerness that went far beyond the normal.

But now that I had finished, the beauty of the dream vanished. Breathless horror and disgust now filled my heart. Unable to endure the face of the being I had created, I rushed out of the room. For a long time I continued pacing my bedroom. I was unable to settle my mind to sleep.

At last, exhaustion replaced the **frenzy** I had before endured. I threw myself on the bed, trying to find a few moments of forgetfulness.

But it was useless. I slept, indeed. But I was disturbed by the wildest dreams. I thought I saw Elizabeth, in the bloom of health, walking in the streets of Ingolstadt. Delighted and surprised, I embraced her.

But as I set the first kiss on her lips, they became pale with the color of death. Her features appeared to change. I thought that I held the **corpse** of my dead mother in my arms. A shroud[2] covered her form. I saw the grave-worms crawling in the folds of the cloth.

I started from my sleep with horror. A cold sweat covered my forehead, my teeth chattered, and every limb shook.

Then the dim and yellow light of the moon forced its way through the window shutters. By it I caught sight of the wretch—the miserable monster whom I had created. He held up the curtain of the bed. His eyes—if they may

---

[2] A shroud is a cloth used to wrap a body for burial.

be called eyes—were fixed on me.

His jaws opened, and he muttered some meaningless sounds. A grin wrinkled his cheeks. He might have spoken, but I didn't hear. One hand was stretched out, seemingly to hold me back. But I escaped and rushed downstairs.

I took refuge in the courtyard of the house in which I lived. There I remained for the rest of the night. I nervously walked up and down, listening closely. I feared each sound might announce the approach of the devilish corpse to which I had so miserably given life.

Oh! No human being could imagine the horror of that face. A mummy given life again couldn't be so **hideous** as that wretch. I had gazed on him while unfinished. He was ugly then. But at last those muscles and joints were able to move. It had become a thing such as even Dante[3] couldn't have imagined.

I passed the night in misery. Sometimes my pulse beat so quickly and strongly that I felt the throbbing of every artery. At others, I nearly sank to the ground from depression and extreme weakness.

I felt the bitterness of disappointment mixed with this horror. My dreams had been my food and pleasant rest for so long. But now they had become a hell to me. And the change was so quick, the overthrow so complete!

Morning at last dawned, dismal and wet. It uncovered to my sleepless and aching eyes the church of Ingolstadt with its white steeple. Its clock indicated the sixth hour.

The porter opened the gates of the court, which had been my shelter that night. I went out into the streets, walking with quick steps. It was as if I were trying to avoid the wretch. I feared that every turning of the street would bring him into view.

I didn't dare return to my apartment. I felt an urge to hurry on, although I was drenched by the rain which

---

[3] Dante Alighieri (1265-1321) was an Italian poet. His most famous work is "The Divine Comedy." The first part of this, "The Inferno," is a description of Hell.

poured from a black and comfortless sky.
I continued walking in this manner for some time. I
tried by bodily exercise to ease the load that weighed
upon my mind. I wandered the streets. I had no clear idea
of where I was or what I was doing. My heart beat in the
sickness of fear. I hurried on with uneven steps, not
daring to look about me:

Like one who, on a lonely road,
Does walk in fear and dread,
And, having once turned round, walks on,
And turns no more his head;
Because he knows a frightful **fiend**
Does close behind him tread.[4]

Continuing thus, I found myself opposite the inn
where the stagecoaches and carriages usually stopped.
Here I paused, I didn't know why. But I remained for
some minutes with my eyes fixed on a coach that was
coming towards me from the other end of the street.

As it drew nearer I observed that it was the Swiss
stagecoach. It stopped just where I was standing, and the
door opened. I caught sight of Henry Clerval, who saw
me and instantly sprung out.

"My dear Frankenstein," he exclaimed, "how glad I
am to see you! How fortunate that you should be here at
the very moment of my arrival!"

Nothing could equal my delight on seeing Clerval. His
presence brought back my father and Elizabeth to my
thoughts. It brought back all those scenes of home so
dear to my memory.

I grasped his hand. In a moment I forgot my horror
and misfortune. For the first time during many months, I
felt a calm and quiet joy. Therefore, I welcomed my
friend in the most **cordial** manner. We walked towards my
college.

---

[4] This excerpt is an adaptation from Samuel Taylor Coleridge's poem "The
Rime of the Ancient Mariner."

Clerval continued talking for some time about our friends. He told me of his own good fortune in being permitted to come to Ingolstadt.

"You may easily believe," he said, "how difficult it was to persuade my father. He thought that no necessary knowledge was to be found outside of the noble art of bookkeeping.

"And indeed, I think I left him unbelieving to the end. For his constant answer to my untiring pleas was always the same. It was that of the Dutch schoolmaster in *The Vicar of Wakefield:* 'I have ten thousand florins a year without Greek. I eat heartily without Greek.'[5]

"But his affection for me finally overcame his dislike of learning. So he has permitted me to undertake a voyage of discovery. Thus I'm off to the land of knowledge."

"It gives me the greatest delight to see you," I replied. "But tell me how you left my father, brothers, and Elizabeth."

"Very well, and very happy. But they are a little worried because they hardly ever hear from you. By the by, I mean to lecture you a little on their behalf myself.

"But my dear Frankenstein," he continued, stopping short and gazing full in my face. "I didn't before remark how very ill you appear. You're so thin and pale. You look as if you had been up for several nights."

"You have guessed right," said I. "I have been deeply engaged in one occupation. And as you can see, I haven't allowed myself enough rest. But I hope—I sincerely hope—that all these employments are now at an end. Perhaps I am at last free."

I trembled greatly. I couldn't bear to think of the occurrences of the night before. I couldn't even imagine them. I walked with a quick pace, and we soon arrived at my college.

---

[5] *The Vicar of Wakefield* is a novel by Oliver Goldsmith (1731-1774). In British currency, a florin was a silver coin worth two shillings, or one-tenth of a pound.

I then considered that the creature whom I had left in my apartment might still be there. He might be alive and walking about. The thought made me shiver. I dreaded to set my eyes on this monster. But I feared more that Henry should see him.

Therefore, I asked him to remain a few minutes at the bottom of the stairs. I darted up towards my own room. My hand was already on the lock of the door before I pulled myself together. I then paused, and a cold shivering came over me.

I threw the door with great force. Children do this when they expect a ghost to be waiting for them on the other side. But nothing appeared.

I stepped fearfully in. The apartment was empty. My bedroom was also freed from its hideous guest. I could hardly believe that such great fortune could be mine. I soon became assured that my enemy had indeed fled. I clapped my hands for joy and ran to Clerval.

We went up into my room, and the servant soon brought breakfast. But I was unable to contain myself. It wasn't only joy that possessed me. I felt my flesh tingle. My pulse beat rapidly. I was unable to remain for a single instant in the same place. I jumped over the chairs, clapped my hands, and laughed aloud.

Clerval at first credited my unusual spirits to joy on his arrival. But then he watched me more closely. He saw a wildness in my eyes which he didn't understand. And my loud, uncontrolled, heartless laughter frightened and astonished him.

"My dear Victor," cried he, "what, for God's sake, is the matter? Don't laugh in that way. How ill you are! What is the cause of all this?"

"Don't ask me," cried I. I put my hands before my eyes, for I thought I saw the dreaded being glide into the room. *"He* can tell. Oh, save me! Save me!"

I imagined that the monster seized me. I struggled furiously and fell down in a fit.

Poor Clerval! What must have been his feelings? He

had looked forward to our meeting with such joy. Now it had so strangely turned to bitterness. But I never witnessed his grief. I fainted and didn't recover my senses for a long, long time. This was the beginning of a nervous fever which kept me in bed for several months. During all that time Henry was my only nurse. He knew my father's advanced age and unfitness for so long a journey. And he knew how miserable my sickness would make Elizabeth. I afterwards learned that he spared them this grief by covering up how sick I really was.

Henry knew that I couldn't have a more kind and attentive nurse than himself. He had firm hopes of my recovery. So he didn't doubt that he was doing no harm. Instead, he performed the kindest action that he could towards my family.

But I was in reality very ill. Surely nothing but the unlimited and unending attentions of my friend could have restored me to life. The form of the monster to whom I had given life was forever before my eyes. I **babbled** nonstop about him.

No doubt my words surprised Henry. He at first believed them to be the wanderings of my disturbed imagination. But I continually repeated the same words with great stubbornness. This persuaded him that my illness had been caused by some unusual and terrible event.

I recovered very slowly. But I alarmed and grieved my friend by falling ill again several times. I remember the first time I became able to look at objects with any kind of pleasure. I noticed that the fallen leaves had disappeared. The young buds were shooting forth from the trees that shaded my window.

It was a heavenly spring. The season sped my recovery. I again felt feelings of joy and affection in my bosom. My gloom disappeared. In a short time I became as cheerful as before I was attacked by the wild passion.

"Dearest Clerval," exclaimed I, "how kind, how very

good you are to me. You had promised yourself that this whole winter would be spent in study. Instead, it has been taken up in my sick room.

"How shall I ever repay you?" I went on. "I feel the greatest regret for the disappointment which I have caused you. I hope you will forgive me."

"You will repay me entirely if you don't worry yourself," said Clerval. "Get well as fast as you can. And since you appear in such good spirits, I may speak to you on one subject, may I not?"

I trembled. One subject! What could it be? Could he refer to an object I didn't dare even think of?

"Calm yourself," said Clerval, who observed my change of color. "I won't mention it if it upsets you. But your father and cousin would be very happy if they received a letter from you in your own handwriting. They hardly know how ill you've been. They're uneasy at your long silence."

"Is that all, my dear Henry?" said I. "How could you suppose that my first thought wouldn't fly towards them? They are my dear, dear friends whom I love and who are so deserving of my love."

"If that is how you feel, my friend," said Henry, "you will perhaps be glad to see a letter that has been lying here some days for you. It's from your cousin, I believe."

Chapter 6 (Summary)

The letter Clerval handed to Frankenstein was indeed from Elizabeth. In it she expressed hopes that his health was improving. She also shared news of Frankenstein's family. She said that Frankenstein's father was well and eager for his return. His sixteen-year-old brother, Ernest, was thinking about a military career. And his smallest brother, William, was growing taller all the time.

Elizabeth also reminded Victor of how fond he had always been of Justine Moritz. Justine was the family servant woman. Elizabeth reminded Victor of how Justine first came to their home. Justine's mother had mistreated her, so the Frankensteins had taken her in. There Justine was treated more as a member of the family than as a servant.

As time passed, all of Justine's brothers and sisters died. Her mother was ill and all alone. Justine returned to her mother's home to help her through her final illness. After her mother died, Justine returned to live with the Frankensteins again.

Elizabeth expressed her desire to hear from Frankenstein as soon as possible. So Frankenstein wrote to her right away.

Frankenstein's terrible experience left him with a strong dislike for science. Clerval sensed this and put Frankenstein's scientific instruments out of sight. But Frankenstein was reminded of his work in other ways.

One day, Frankenstein introduced Clerval to Professors Waldman and Krempe. Both professors praised Frankenstein highly to his friend. This praise only made Frankenstein feel worse about what he had done.

Clerval began to study Oriental languages. Frankenstein also took up these studies, partly as a way to forget science. The summer passed as they studied together.

Frankenstein hoped to return to Geneva late that fall.

But the weather made a journey impossible. He had to wait until the following spring. May came, and Frankenstein was ready to go home. But before he went, Clerval took him on a walking tour. They traveled through the countryside around Ingolstadt. Frankenstein greatly enjoyed the beautiful scenery and Clerval's company. He was very grateful to Clerval for bringing him back to life again.

Chapter 7

On my return to the college from my walk, I found the following letter from my father:

My dear Victor:
    You have probably waited impatiently for a letter to fix the date of your return to us. I was at first tempted to write only a few lines. I hoped merely to mention the day on which I should expect you.
    But that would be a cruel kindness, and I dare not do it. You would arrive expecting a happy and glad welcome. What would be your surprise, my son, to find, instead, tears and misery?
    And how, Victor, can I tell you our misfortune? Absence can't have made you **callous** to our joys and griefs. How shall I inflict pain on my long-absent son?
    I wish to prepare you for the awful news, but I know it's impossible. Even now your eye skims over the page. You look for the words which are to tell you the horrible news.
    William is dead! That sweet child, whose smiles

delighted and warmed my heart, who was so gentle, yet so lively! Victor, he is murdered!

I won't try to comfort you. I will simply relate the circumstances of how it happened.

Last Thursday (May 7th) I, my niece, and your two brothers went to walk in Plainpalais. The evening was warm and calm. So we took our walk farther than usual. It was already dusk before we thought of returning. Then we discovered that William and Ernest, who had gone on before, weren't to be found. We therefore rested on a seat until they should return.

Presently, Ernest came and inquired if we had seen his brother. He said that he had been playing with him. William had run away to hide himself. Then Ernest had looked for him in vain, and afterwards waited for him a long time. But he didn't return.

This account rather alarmed us. We continued to search for him until night fell. Then Elizabeth guessed that he might have returned to the house. He wasn't there.

We returned again with torches. I couldn't rest when I thought that my sweet boy had lost himself and was out in the damps and dews of night. Elizabeth also suffered extreme anguish.

About five in the morning I discovered my lovely boy. The night before I had seen him blooming and active in health. Now he was stretched on the grass, pale and motionless. The print of the murderer's finger was on his neck.

He was taken home. The anguish that was visible in my face betrayed the secret to Elizabeth. She was determined to see the corpse. At first I tried to prevent her. But she insisted.

She entered the room where it lay. She quickly examined the neck of the victim and clasped her hands.

"Oh, God!" she exclaimed. "I have murdered my darling child!"

She fainted and was restored with great difficulty.

When she was again conscious, it was only to weep and sigh.

She told me something which had happened that same evening. William had persuaded her to let him wear a very valuable miniature of your mother that she had. This picture is gone. It was doubtless the temptation which urged the murderer to do the deed.

We have no trace of him yet, although our attempts to discover him are tireless. But they won't restore my beloved William!

Come, dearest Victor. You alone can comfort Elizabeth. She weeps continually and falsely accuses herself as the cause of his death. Her words pierce my heart. We are all unhappy. But won't that be an additional reason for you, my son, to return and be our comforter?

Your dear mother! Alas, Victor! I now say, thank God she didn't live to witness the cruel, miserable death of her youngest darling.

Come, Victor. But don't bring thoughts of revenge against the **assassin.** Bring feelings of peace and gentleness. Come to heal the wounds of our minds, not inflame them.

Enter the house of mourning, my friend. But bring kindness for those who love you. Don't bring hatred for your enemies.

Your affectionate and grieving father,
Alphonse Frankenstein
Geneva, May 12th, 17—

Clerval had watched my face as I read this letter. I had at first shown joy on receiving news from my friends. But he was surprised to observe the despair that came after it. I threw the letter on the table and covered my face with my hands.

"My dear Frankenstein," exclaimed Henry when he saw me weep with bitterness. "Are you always to be unhappy? My dear friend, what has happened?"

I motioned to him to take up the letter. In the

meantime, I walked up and down the room in the most extreme agitation. Tears also gushed from the eyes of Clerval as he read the account of my misfortune. "I can offer you no comfort, my friend," said he. "Your disaster is beyond repair. What do you intend to do?" "To go instantly to Geneva," said I. "Come with me to order the horses, Henry."

During our walk, Clerval attempted to say a few words of comfort. But he could only express his heartfelt sympathy.

"Poor William!" said he. "Dear lovely child, he now sleeps with his angel mother! We had seen him bright and joyous in his young beauty. Now we must weep over his untimely loss!

"To die so miserably, to feel the murderer's grasp!" exclaimed Clerval. "How cruel to destroy such shining innocence! Poor little fellow!

"We have only one comfort," he continued. "His friends mourn and weep, but he is at rest. The pain is over. His sufferings are at an end forever. Earth covers his gentle form, and he knows no pain. He can no longer be a subject for pity. We must save that for his miserable survivors."

Clerval spoke thus as we hurried through the streets. The words impressed themselves on my mind. I remembered them afterwards when I was alone. But now, as soon as the horses arrived, I hurried into a carriage. I bade farewell to my friend.

My journey was very gloomy. At first I wished to hurry on. I longed to comfort and sympathize with my loved and sorrowing friends. But when I drew near my native town, I slowed. I could hardly deal with the many questions that crowded into my mind.

I passed through scenes from my youth. I hadn't seen them for nearly six years. How changed everything might be during that time! True, one sudden and terrible change had taken place. But a thousand little things, little by little, might have worked other changes. Although they may have been done more quietly, they were still changes.

Fear overcame me. I dared not go farther. I dreaded a thousand evils that made me tremble. But I was unable to name these evils.

I remained two days at Lausanne in this painful state of mind. I gazed upon the lake. The waters were peaceful, and all around was calm. The snowy mountains, "the palaces of nature," weren't changed.

Gradually the calm and heavenly scene restored me. I continued my journey towards Geneva.

The road ran by the side of the lake and became narrower as I approached my hometown. I saw more clearly the black sides of Jura and the bright peak of Mont Blanc. I wept like a child.

"Dear mountains!" I cried. "My own beautiful lake! How do you welcome your wanderer? Your tops are clear. The sky and lake are blue and calm. Is this to tell of peace or to laugh at my unhappiness?"

I fear, my friend, that I shall become dull by retelling these early circumstances. But they were days of comparative happiness, and I think of them with pleasure.

My country, my beloved country! I beheld your streams, your mountains, and more than all, your lovely lake! Who else but a native can tell the delight I took in all these things?

Yet, as I drew nearer home, grief and fear again overcame me. Night also closed around. When I could hardly see the dark mountains, I felt still more gloomy.

The picture appeared a huge and dim scene of evil. I vaguely saw that I was about to become the most miserable of human beings.

Alas! I predicted correctly. I failed only in one single circumstance. True, I imagined and dreaded great misery. But I didn't imagine the hundredth part of the pain and sorrow I was going to endure.

It was completely dark when I arrived in the outskirts of Geneva. The gates of the town were already shut. I was forced to pass the night at Secheron. This was a village at the distance of half a league[1] from the city. The sky was calm. As I was unable to rest, I decided to visit the spot where my poor William had been murdered. I couldn't pass through the town. So I needed to cross the lake in a boat to arrive at Plainpalais. During this short voyage I saw the lightning play on the peak of Mont Blanc. It formed the most beautiful figures. The storm appeared to approach quickly. On landing, I climbed a low hill so that I might observe its progress.

It advanced. The heavens were clouded. I soon felt the rain coming slowly in large drops, but its violence quickly increased.

I left my seat and walked on. The darkness and storm increased every minute. The thunder burst with a terrific crash over my head. It was echoed from Salêve, the Juras, and the Alps of Savoy.

Brilliant flashes of lightning dazzled my eyes. They lit up the lake, making it appear like a great sheet of fire. Then for an instant everything seemed pitch black, until the eye recovered from the flash before.

The storm appeared at once in different parts of the heavens. This is often the case in Switzerland. The most violent storm hung exactly north of town. It was above that part of the lake which lies between the cape of Belrive and the village of Copêt. Another storm enlightened Jura with faint flashes. Another darkened and sometimes disclosed the Môle, a peaked mountain to the east of the lake.

The storm was beautiful, yet so violent. While I watched it, I wandered on with a quick step. This noble war in the sky raised my spirits.

I clasped my hands and exclaimed aloud, "William,

---

[1] A league usually refers to a distance of about three miles.

dear angel! This is your funeral, this your dirge!"[2]
As I said these words, I caught sight of a figure in the dark. It stole from behind a clump of trees near me. I stood still, gazing intently. I couldn't be mistaken. A flash of lightning lit up the object and displayed its shape plainly to me. It was of gigantic size, and its shape was deformed. It was too hideous to be anything human. I could instantly see that it was the wretch, the filthy demon to whom I had given life.

What was he doing there? Could he be my brother's murderer? I **shuddered** at the idea. But no sooner did it cross my imagination than I became convinced of its truth. My teeth chattered, and I was forced to lean against a tree for support. The figure passed me quickly, and I lost it in the gloom.

Nothing in human shape could have destroyed that fair child. *He* was the murderer! I couldn't doubt it. Just the idea of it proved the fact.

I thought of going after the devil, but it would have been in vain. Another flash showed him to me. He was hanging among the rocks of the nearby steep sides of Mont Salêve, a hill that bounds Plainpalais on the south. He soon reached the top and disappeared.

I remained motionless. The thunder stopped, but the rain still continued. The scene was surrounded by the deepest darkness. I turned over in my mind the events which I had until now tried to forget.

I traced the whole path of my progress towards the creation of my work. I remembered it standing alive at my bedside and its departure.

Nearly two years had now gone by since the night on which he first received life. Was this his first crime? Alas! I had turned loose into the world a cruel wretch whose delight was in destruction and misery. Hadn't he murdered my brother?

No one can imagine the pain I suffered during the

---

[2] A dirge is a mournful song, often sang at funerals.

remainder of the night. I spent it cold and wet in the open air. But I didn't feel the discomfort of the weather. My imagination was busy in scenes of evil and despair. I thought about the being whom I had cast among mankind. He had been given the will and power to carry out deeds of horror. He had just done such a deed. He seemed almost like my own vampire, my own spirit let loose from the grave. And now he was forced to destroy all that was dear to me.

Day dawned, and I turned toward the town. The town gates were open, and I hurried to my father's house. My first thought was to tell what I knew of the murderer. This would cause instant pursuit to be made.

But I paused when I reflected on the story I had to tell. I had formed a being and given it life. He had met me at midnight among the cliffs of an unclimbable mountain.

I remembered also my nervous fever. I had been seized by it just at the time that I dated my creation. This would give an air of **delirium** to a tale otherwise so very unlikely. I well knew what I would think if anyone else had told such a story to me. I should have thought that person mad.

Besides, the strange nature of the animal would escape all pursuit. It wouldn't matter if I were so much believed as to persuade my relatives to go after it. What use would that be? Who could stop a creature that could climb the overhanging sides of Mont Salêve?

These reflections made my decision for me. I resolved to remain silent.

It was about five in the morning when I entered my father's house. I told the servants not to disturb the family. I went into the library to wait for their usual hour of rising.

Six years had gone by. They had passed as a dream but for one certain trace. At last, I stood again in the same place where I had embraced my father before my departure for Ingolstadt.

Beloved and respected parent! He still remained so to

me. I gazed on the picture of my mother which stood over the mantelpiece. It was a historical subject, painted at my father's request. The picture represented Caroline Beaufort in an agony of despair. She was kneeling by the coffin of her dead father. Her clothes were plain and her cheek pale. But there was an air of dignity and beauty that hardly permitted any feeling of pity. Below this picture was a miniature of William. My tears flowed when I looked at it.

While I was thus engaged, Ernest entered. He had heard me arrive and hurried to welcome me. He expressed a sorrowful delight to see me.

"Welcome, my dearest Victor," said he. "Ah! I wish you had come three months ago. Then you would have found us all joyous and delighted. You come to us now to share a misery which nothing can ease.

"Yet your presence will revive our father, I hope. He seems to be sinking under his misfortune. And you will persuade poor Elizabeth to end her vain and tormenting self-accusations. Poor William! He was our darling and our pride!"

Tears fell from my brother's eyes, and he didn't try to stop them. A sense of horrible agony crept over me. Before, I had only imagined the misery of my ruined home. The reality was no less terrible.

I tried to calm Ernest. Then I asked for more details of my father and Elizabeth.

"She, most of all, requires comfort," said Ernest. "She accused herself of having caused my brother's death. That has made her very heartsick. But since the murderer has been discovered—"

"The murderer discovered!" I cried. "Good God! How can that be? Who could even try to go after him? It's impossible. One might as well try to overtake the winds or enclose a mountain stream with a straw. I saw him too. He was free last night!"

"I don't know what you mean," replied my brother

with a note of wonder. "But to us, the discovery we have made completes our misery. No one would believe it at first. And even now Elizabeth won't be convinced, in spite of all the evidence.

"Indeed," Ernest continued, "who would believe that Justine Moritz could suddenly become capable of so frightful, so dreadful a crime? She, who was so kind and fond of all the family!"

"Justine Moritz!" said I. "Poor, poor girl, is she the accused? But it is wrongfully so. Everyone knows that. No one believes it, surely, Ernest?"

"No one did at first," replied my brother. "But several circumstances have come out. These have almost forced us to believe in her guilt. Her own confused behavior has added a great deal of weight to the evidence of facts. I'm afraid there is no hope for doubt. But she will be tried today, and you will then hear all."

Ernest related what had happened. On the morning poor William's murder had been discovered, Justine had been taken ill. She had to stay in her bed for several days.

During this time, one of the servants happened to examine the clothing Justine had worn on the night of the murder. She discovered in Justine's pocket the picture of my mother. This was the picture that was thought to be the murderer's temptation.

The servant instantly showed it to one of the others. Without saying a word to any of the family, they went to a magistrate.[3] As a result, Justine was arrested and charged with the murder. The poor girl's confused manner confirmed the suspicion in great measure.

This was a strange tale, but it didn't shake my faith. I replied earnestly, "You are all mistaken. I know the murderer. Justine, poor, good Justine, is innocent."

At that instant my father entered. I saw unhappiness deeply impressed on his face. But he tried hard to welcome me cheerfully.

---

[3] A magistrate is a local official who oversees legal matters.

When we had exchanged our mournful greeting, my father tried to introduce some other topic than that of our disaster. But Ernest exclaimed, "Good God, Papa! Victor says that he knows who murdered poor William."

"We do also, unfortunately," replied my father. "Indeed, I would rather never have found out the truth. To have discovered so much wickedness and ungratefulness in one I thought so highly of!"

"My dear father, you are mistaken," said I. "Justine is innocent."

"If she is, God forbid that she should suffer as guilty," said my father. "She is to be tried today. I hope—I sincerely hope—that she will be found innocent."

This speech calmed me. I was firmly convinced in my own mind that Justine was guiltless of this murder. Indeed, every human being was innocent as well. Therefore, I had no fear of any circumstantial evidence.[4] Surely none could be brought forward strong enough to convict her.

My tale was not one to announce publicly. Its shocking horror would be looked upon as madness by the average person.

Did anyone indeed exist who could believe the truth? None, surely, unless real proof of the creature's existence showed him. Only I, the creator, could grasp the horror. I knew I had let loose upon the world a living reminder of pride and careless ignorance.

We were soon joined by Elizabeth. Time had changed her since I last saw her. It had brought her loveliness greater than the beauty of her childish years. There was the same openness, the same liveliness. But it was mixed with an expression more full of intelligence and common sense. She welcomed me with the greatest affection.

"My dear cousin," said she, "your arrival fills me with hope. You perhaps will find some means to help my poor guiltless Justine. Alas! Who is safe, if someone like

---

[4] Circumstantial evidence is information that can be used against a defendant but—when used alone—doesn't prove guilt.

Justine be convicted of crime? I'm as sure of her innocence as certainly as I am my own.

"Our misfortune is doubly hard on us," Elizabeth went on. "We've already lost that lovely darling boy. But now this poor girl, whom I sincerely love, is to be torn away by an even worse fate.

If she is condemned, I never shall know joy again. But she won't be. I am sure she won't be. And then I shall be happy again, even after the sad death of my little William."

"She is innocent, my Elizabeth," said I. "And that shall be proved. Fear nothing, but let your spirits be cheered. For she shall certainly not be found guilty."

"How kind and generous you are!" Elizabeth exclaimed. "Everyone else believes in her guilt. That made me miserable, for I knew that it was impossible. To see everyone else **biased** in so deadly a manner made me hopeless and despairing." She wept.

"Dearest niece," said my father, "dry your tears. If she is innocent, as you believe, depend on the justice of our laws. I shall do all I can to prevent the slightest unfairness."

Chapter 8

Vocabulary Preview

The following words appear in this chapter.
Review the list and get to know the words
before you read the chapter.

acquit—declare innocent; set free
besieged—pressured
ingratitude—thanklessness; ungratefulness
merit—excellence; goodness
prophetic—foretelling; predicting
solemnity—seriousness
spectators—onlookers; watchers

We passed a few sad hours until eleven o'clock, when the trial was to begin. My father and the rest of the family needed to attend as witnesses. I went with them to the court.

During the whole awful mockery of justice, I suffered living torture. For the result of my curiosity and lawless activities was to be decided there.

It might prove to be the death of two of my fellow beings. One was a smiling babe full of innocence and joy. The other would be far more dreadfully murdered. All possible shame and disgrace of that murder would make its horror long remembered.

Justine was a girl of **merit.** She had qualities which promised to make her life happy. Now all was to be forgotten in a dishonored grave. And I was the cause!

A thousand times I would rather have confessed myself guilty of the murder. But I was absent when it was committed. And such a confession would have been seen as the confused babbling of a madman. It would have been no help to her who suffered because of me.

Justine appeared calm. She was dressed in mourning. And her face—always attractive—was made perfectly beautiful by the **solemnity** of her feelings.

In her innocence, she appeared confident and didn't tremble. Yet she was gazed on and accused by thousands. Once, her beauty might have inspired great kindness. But the **spectators** forgot all about kindness. All they could think of was the outrage she was supposed to have committed.

She was calm, but her calmness seemed forced. Her confusion had before been taken as a proof of her guilt. So she worked up her mind to an appearance of courage.

When she entered the court she threw her eyes round it. She quickly found where we were seated. A tear seemed to dim her eye when she saw us. But she quickly recovered. A look of sorrowful affection seemed to prove to us her complete innocence.

The trial began. After the prosecuting attorney[1] had stated the charge, some witnesses were called. Several strange facts were put together against her. These might have convinced anyone who didn't have such proof of her innocence as I had.

She had been out the whole of the night on which the murder had been committed. Towards morning she had been seen by a market woman. This hadn't been far from the spot where the body of the murdered child had later been found.

The woman had asked her what she did there. But Justine looked very strange and only gave a confused and meaningless answer.

Justine returned to the house about eight o'clock in the morning. When anyone asked where she had spent the night, she replied that she had been looking for the child. She demanded earnestly if there was any news of

---

[1] A prosecuting attorney is a lawyer who tries to prove the accused is guilty.

him. When shown the body, she fell into violent fits. She kept to her bed for several days.

The picture was then produced which the servant had found in Justine's pocket. In a sad voice, Elizabeth said that it was the same one she had put around the child's neck. She had done so an hour before the child had been missed. At Elizabeth's words, a murmur of horror and anger filled the court.

Justine was called on for her defense. As the trial had proceeded, her face had changed. Surprise, horror, and misery were strongly shown.

Sometimes she struggled with her tears. But when she was asked to plead, she pulled herself together. She spoke in a clear but shaking voice.

"God knows how entirely innocent I am," she said. "But I don't pretend that my words of protest should convince you to **acquit** me. I rest my innocence on a plain and simple explanation of the facts brought against me.

"Sometimes their circumstances appear doubtful or suspicious. I hope my good character will convince my judges to see them in a favorable way."

Justine then told what had happened. She had passed the evening of the night of the murder at an aunt's house at Chêne. This was a village located about a league from Geneva. She had done so with Elizabeth's permission.

On her return at about nine o'clock, she met a man. He asked her if she had seen anything of the child who was lost. She was alarmed at this and spent several hours in looking for him.

Then the gates of Geneva were shut. She was forced to spend several hours of the night in a barn belonging to a cottage. She was unwilling to wake up the people who lived there, as they knew her well.

Most of the night she spent there watching. She believed that she slept for a few minutes towards morning. Some steps disturbed her, and she awoke.

It was dawn, and she left her resting place. She again tried to find my brother. If she had gone near the spot

where his body lay, she hadn't been aware of it.
True, she had been confused when questioned by the
market woman. But this wasn't surprising. She had passed
a sleepless night, and poor William's fate was still
unknown. She knew nothing of the picture William had
been wearing.

"I know," continued the unhappy victim, "how
heavily and fatally this one detail weighs against me. But
I have no way of explaining it. I must express my
complete ignorance. I am only left to guess when it might
have been placed in my pocket.

"But here also I am checked. I believe that I have no
enemy on earth. I surely have none so wicked as to
destroy me on purpose. Did the murderer place the
locket there? I don't know when he could have done it.
Even if I did know, why should he have stolen the jewel,
only to give it up again so soon?

"I turn over my cause to the justice of my judges. Yet
I see no room for hope. I beg permission to have a few
witnesses examined about my character. I hope their
words shall outweigh my supposed guilt.

"If not," Justine continued, "I must be condemned.
But I would pledge my freedom on my innocence."

Several witnesses were called who had known her for
many years. They spoke well of her. But they, too, were
full of fear and hatred of the crime which they thought
her guilty of. As a result, they were afraid and unwilling
to come forward.

Elizabeth realized that Justine's excellent nature and
perfect behavior were her last defense. But even these
were about to fail the accused. Though violently upset,
Elizabeth asked permission to address the court.

"I am the cousin of the unhappy child who was
murdered," she began. "Or rather, I am his sister. For I
was educated by and have lived with his parents since
long before his birth.

"Therefore, it may be judged improper of me to come
forward at this time. But I see a fellow creature about to

perish through the cowardice of her so-called friends. And I wish to be allowed to speak. I want to say what I know of her character.

"I know the accused well. I have lived in the same house with her—at one time for five years and at another for nearly two years.

"During all that time, Justine appeared to me the most friendly and kindly creature. She nursed Madame Frankenstein, my aunt, in her last illness. She did so with the greatest affection and care.

"Afterwards," continued Elizabeth, "she cared for her own mother during a difficult illness. Her manner at that time gained the admiration of all who knew her. Then she again lived in my uncle's house. She was beloved there by all the family.

"Justine was warmly attached to the child who is now dead. She acted towards him like a most affectionate mother. For my part, I believe and have faith in her perfect innocence. I don't hesitate to say this, in spite of all the evidence produced against her. She had no temptation for such an action.

"The trinket on which the main proof rests proves nothing. If she had really wanted it, I should have given it to her willingly. That's how much I respect and value her."

A murmur of approval followed Elizabeth's simple and powerful plea. But this murmur was inspired by her generous action. It was not in favor of poor Justine. The public's anger turned upon her again with renewed violence. It charged her with the worst **ingratitude.** Justine wept as Elizabeth spoke, but she didn't answer.

My own worry and pain were extreme during the whole trial. I believed in her innocence. I knew it. I didn't doubt for a minute that the demon had murdered my brother. Did he also in his hellish game send the innocent to death and dishonor?

I soon understood the popular voice and the faces of the judges. They had already condemned my unhappy victim. I couldn't bear the horror of my situation, and I rushed out of the court in agony.

The tortures of the accused did not equal mine. Justine was held up by innocence. But the fangs of remorse tore at me and wouldn't let go. I spent the night in complete misery. In the morning, I went to court. My lips and throat were dry. I didn't dare ask the deadly question. But I was recognized, and the officer guessed why I was there.

The ballots had been thrown. They were all black, and Justine was condemned.

I can't pretend to describe what I then felt. I had experienced sensations of horror before. And I have tried to express my feelings adequately. But words can't describe the heart-sickening despair that I then endured.

The person to whom I spoke added that Justine had already confessed her guilt. "That evidence," he observed, "was hardly required in such a clear case. But I'm glad of it. Indeed, none of our judges like to condemn a criminal on circumstantial evidence, no matter how certain."

This was strange and unexpected news. What could it mean? Had my eyes fooled me? And what if I explained what I really suspected? Would I really be as mad as the whole world would believe me to be? I hurried home. Elizabeth eagerly demanded the result.

"My cousin," replied I, "it is decided as you may have expected. All judges would rather ten innocent people should suffer than one guilty should escape. But Justine has confessed!"

This was a serious blow to poor Elizabeth. She had put such firm faith upon Justine's innocence.

"Alas!" said she. "How shall I ever again believe in human goodness? I loved and honored Justine as my sister. How could she put on those smiles of innocence only to betray? Her mild eyes didn't seem capable of any cruelty or trickery. And yet she has committed a murder."

Soon after, we heard that the poor victim had asked to see my cousin. My father didn't want Elizabeth to go.

But he said that he left the decision up to her.

"Yes," said Elizabeth. "I will go, although she is guilty. And you, Victor, shall accompany me. I can't go alone."

The thought of this visit was torture to me. Yet I couldn't refuse.

We entered the gloomy prison chamber. There we found Justine sitting on some straw at the farther end. Her hands were bound, and her head rested on her knees. She rose on seeing us enter. When we were left alone with her, she threw herself at Elizabeth's feet, weeping bitterly. My cousin wept also.

"Oh, Justine!" said she. "Why did you rob me of my last hope? I was so certain of your innocence. Although I was very unhappy, I wasn't so miserable as I am now."

"And do you also believe that I am so very, very wicked?" cried Justine. "Do you also join with my enemies to crush me? To condemn me as a murderer?"

Her voice was choked with sobs.

"Rise, my poor girl," said Elizabeth. "Why do you kneel, if you are innocent? I'm not one of your enemies. I believed you guiltless, in spite of every evidence.

"But then I heard that you yourself had declared your guilt," Elizabeth continued. "That report, you say, is false. Be assured, dear Justine, that only your own confession can shake my confidence in you for a moment. Nothing else can do it."

"I did confess," replied Justine. "But I confessed a lie. I confessed so that I might obtain forgiveness. But now that falsehood lies heavier on my heart than all my other sins.

"The God of heaven forgive me! Ever since I was condemned, my confessor[2] has **besieged** me. He threatened and terrorized me. At last I almost began to think that I was the monster that he said I was. He threatened excommunication[3] and hell fire in my last

---

[2] A confessor is a priest.
[3] Excommunication is punishment for not following the rules of a religion. The offender is banned from church membership.

moments if I continued to be stubborn.

"Dear lady," continued Justine, "I had no one to support me. All looked on me as a wretch doomed to dishonor and damnation. What could I do? In an evil hour I gave in to a lie. And it is only now that I am truly miserable."

She paused, weeping, and then continued, "I thought with horror, my sweet lady, that you should believe such a thing of me. Your blessed aunt had highly honored me, and you had loved me. I couldn't have you believe me a creature capable of such a crime. Only the devil himself could have committed such an act.

"Dear William! Dearest blessed child! I soon shall see you again in heaven, where we shall all be happy. And that comforts me, going as I am to suffer shame and death."

"Oh, Justine!" said Elizabeth. "Forgive me for having distrusted you for one moment. Why did you confess? But do not mourn, dear girl. Don't fear. I will proclaim, I will prove your innocence. I'll melt the stony hearts of your enemies by my tears and prayers.

"You shall not die!" Elizabeth went on. "You, my playmate, my companion, my sister, perish on the scaffold? No! No! I could never survive so horrible a misfortune!"

Justine shook her head mournfully.

"I'm not scared of dying," she said. "That pain is past. God raises my weakness and gives me courage to endure the worst.

"I leave a sad and bitter world. Remember me, and think of me as one unfairly condemned. I have accepted the fate awaiting me. Learn from me, dear lady, to accept the will of heaven with patience!"

During this conversation I had retired to a corner of the prison room. There I could hide the horrid suffering that possessed me.

Despair! Who dared talk of that? On the next day, the poor victim would pass the awful boundary between life and death. But she didn't feel—as I did—such deep and bitter agony. I ground my teeth and uttered a groan that came from my inmost soul.

Justine jumped. When she saw who it was, she approached me and said, "Dear sir, you are very kind to visit me. You, I hope, don't believe that I am guilty?"

I couldn't answer.

"No, Justine," said Elizabeth. "He is more convinced of your innocence than I was. For even when he heard you had confessed, he didn't believe it."

"I truly thank him," said Justine. "In these last moments I feel the sincerest gratitude toward those who think of me with kindness. How sweet is the affection of others to such a wretch as I!

"It removes more than half my misfortune," Justine said. "I feel as if I could die in peace now. At least you, dear lady, and your cousin have declared my innocence."

Thus the poor sufferer tried to comfort others and herself. She indeed gained the peace she desired. But I— the true murderer—felt my grief alive in my bosom. It allowed no hope or comfort.

Elizabeth also wept. But hers also was the misery of innocence. Such misery is like a cloud that passes over a fair moon. For a while it hides but can't dull the moon's brightness. Distress and despair had pierced the core of my heart. There was a hell within me which nothing could end.

We stayed several hours with Justine. It was with great difficulty that Elizabeth could tear herself away.

"I wish," cried Elizabeth, "that I were to die with you. I can't live in this world of misery."

Justine took on a cheerful manner. But she kept back her bitter tears with difficulty. She embraced Elizabeth and spoke in a voice of half-hidden emotion.

"Farewell, sweet lady, dearest Elizabeth," said Justine. "You are my beloved and only friend. May heaven, in its goodness, bless and preserve you. May this be the last misfortune that you will ever suffer! Live, and be happy, and make others so."

And on the next day Justine died. Elizabeth's heart-rending speeches failed to move the judges. They continued to believe in the guilt of the saintly sufferer. My passionate and angry appeals also were lost upon them. I listened to their cold answers. I heard the harsh, unfeeling reasoning of these men. And the truth died away on my lips.

I might call myself a madman. But I couldn't change the sentence passed upon my unhappy victim. She was put to death as a murderess!

My own heart was tortured. But I turned from that to reflect on the deep and voiceless grief of my Elizabeth. This also was my doing! And so was my father's sadness. And the sadness of that home that smiled only so recently. All this was the work of my devilish hands!

You weep, unhappy ones, I thought. But these are not your last tears! Again shall you raise the funeral wail. The sound of your mourning shall again and again be heard!

Victor Frankenstein is your son, your relative, your early, much-loved friend. He would give each drop of blood for your sakes. He has no thought nor sense of joy except when you are also happy. He would fill the air with blessings and spend his life in serving you.

Yet he knows you will continue to weep, to shed countless tears. He would be happy beyond his hopes if this fate should not be satisfied. If only the horror would end before the peace of the grave follows your cries! But he knows it won't be so.

Thus spoke my **prophetic** soul. I was torn by remorse, horror, and despair. I watched those I loved spend useless sorrow on the graves of William and Justine. Those two were the first unlucky victims of my unholy arts.

Chapter 9 (Summary)

Frankenstein was very depressed after Justine's death. The guilt he felt at creating such a horrible monster haunted him. He found it awful to still be alive while an innocent girl was dead. Frankenstein's health began to fail. He spent more and more time alone.

His father couldn't have known why Frankenstein was so troubled. He felt that his son was merely grieving over the recent deaths. Therefore, he tried to soothe Frankenstein. He encouraged him to get on with his life. But Frankenstein was not to be comforted.

The family left Geneva to spend more time at their house at Belrive. While there, Frankenstein spent many long hours boating on the lake. Often he felt like drowning himself. But thoughts of his family always stopped him.

Frankenstein feared that his monster would commit yet another crime. But aside from fear, he also felt anger and hatred. He wanted revenge. He wanted to track down the monster and kill him.

Meanwhile, Frankenstein's family continued to grieve in their own ways. Elizabeth was particularly unhappy. The question of Justine's guilt was always on her mind. She had to believe that Justine was innocent. Otherwise, she could no longer have any faith in humankind.

Elizabeth noticed that Frankenstein was even more unhappy than she. She wished that being around his loved ones would ease his sorrow. Of course, he couldn't explain to her why this wasn't possible.

Some two months after Justine's death, Frankenstein grew restless and in need of exercise. So he wandered off into the nearby Alpine valleys. The sight of ruined castles, huge glaciers,[1] and the high mountain peaks cheered him. When night came, he arrived in the village of Chamounix. He decided to remain there until morning.

---

[1] Glaciers are slow-moving bodies of ice.

Chapter 10

Vocabulary Preview

The following words appear in this chapter. Review the list and get to know the words before you read the chapter.

despise—strongly dislike; hate
spurn—reject; turn away; turn one's back on
stupendous—amazing; out of the ordinary
vengeance—punishment given in return for a wrong done; revenge

I spent the following day roaming through the valley. I stood beside the glaciers near the Arveiron River. The river runs slowly from the top of the hills down into the valley.

The steep sides of great mountains were before me. The icy wall of the glacier hung over me. A few shattered pines were scattered around. There was solemn silence in this glorious presence-chamber[1] of mighty nature.

This silence was rarely broken. Sometimes I could hear the crashing waves or the fall of some great object. Or there might come the thunder sound of the avalanche.[2]

Also, I might hear the cracking of the built-up ice echoing among the mountains. This ice was endlessly cracked and torn due to the silent working of nature. It was as if the ice were but a plaything in nature's hands.

These breathtaking and magnificent scenes gave me the greatest comfort I could receive. They raised my

---

[1] A presence-chamber is a room where an important person receives visitors.
[2] An avalanche is a large mass of falling ice or snow.

spirits. Although they didn't remove my grief, they quieted and eased it. In some degree, they also allowed me to think new thoughts. I had worried too much over the same thoughts for the last month.

At night, I rested. In a way, my sleep was waited on and well cared for. I had looked at the collection of grand shapes during the day. Now they gathered around me and watched over my sleep. There was the unstained snowy mountaintop, the glittering peak, the pine woods, and the ragged, bare ravine.[3] And there also was the eagle, soaring among the clouds. They all grouped round me and helped me be at peace.

Where had they fled when the next morning I awoke? All that had lifted my soul had vanished with sleep. Now, dark sadness clouded every thought.

The rain was pouring in torrents. Thick mists hid the tops of the mountains. I didn't even see the faces of those mighty friends. Still, I'd look through their misty veil and seek them in their cloudy retreats. What were rain and storm to me?

My mule was brought to the door. I decided to climb to the top of Montanvert. I remembered the great effect the tremendous and ever-moving glacier had on my mind when I first saw it. It had then filled me with a great delight. It had given wings to my soul and allowed it to soar from the dark world to light and joy.

Indeed, the sight of the great and majestic in nature always had this effect. They made my mind serious and caused me to forget the passing cares of life. I decided to go without a guide, since I knew the path well. The presence of another person would destroy the lonely grandness of the scene.

The climb is steep. But the path is cut into continual short twists and curves. These enable you to overcome the steepness of the mountain.

It is a very lonely scene. In a thousand spots the traces

---

[3] A ravine is a deep cut in the earth, often made by moving water.

of the winter avalanche may be seen. There the trees lie broken and scattered about on the ground. Some are entirely destroyed. Others are bent, leaning upon the rocks sticking out of the mountain, or lying across other trees. As you climb higher, ravines of snow cut across the path. Stones continually roll down them from above. Any one of these stones is extremely dangerous. The slightest sound must be avoided, such as even speaking in a loud voice. One noise can produce a clap of air strong enough to bring destruction on the head of the speaker. The pines aren't tall or numerous. But they are gloomy and add an air of coldness to the scene.

I looked on the valley below. Great mists were rising from the waters which ran through it. The mists curled in thick wreaths around the mountains on the other side. The mountain peaks were hidden in the shapeless clouds while rain poured from the dark sky. The dreary impression I received from the objects around me grew.

Alas! Why does man boast of a better life than that of the animals? This only makes our feelings harder. Our sensations ought to be limited to hunger, thirst, and desire. Then we might be nearly free. But now we're moved by every wind that blows. We are deeply affected by a chance word—or the scene which that word reminds us of.

We rest; a dream has power to poison sleep.
We rise; one wandering thought pollutes the day.
We feel, think, or reason; laugh or weep,
Embrace fond misery, or cast our cares away.
It is the same: for be it joy or sorrow,
The path of its departure is still free.
Man's yesterday may never be like his tomorrow.
Nothing may endure but the ability to change![4]

---

[4] This is an adaptation of the ending of the poem "Mutability" by Percy Bysshe Shelley.

It was nearly noon when I arrived at the top of my climb. For some time I sat on the rock that overlooks the sea of ice. A mist covered both that and the surrounding mountains. Presently a breeze dissolved the cloud, and I went down to the glacier. The surface is very uneven, rising like the waves of a troubled sea. It descends low and is broken up by deep cracks. The field of ice is almost a league in width, but I spent nearly two hours in crossing it. The opposite mountain is a bare, steep rock. From the side where I now stood, Montanvert was exactly opposite. It was about a league away. Above it rose Mont Blanc in awesome majesty. I remained in a hollow of the rock, gazing on this wonderful and **stupendous** scene.

The sea—or rather, the great river of ice—wound among its surrounding mountains. Their high peaks hung over its hollows. Their icy and glittering tops shone in the sunlight over the clouds.

Before, my heart had been sorrowful. But now it swelled with something like joy. I exclaimed, "Wandering spirits—if indeed you wander, and don't rest in your narrow beds—allow me this brief happiness. Or take me as your companion away from the joys of life."

As I said this I suddenly noticed the figure of a man. He was some distance away, coming towards me with superhuman speed. He bounded over the cracks in the ice, where I had walked with such caution before. His size, also, as he approached, seemed to be greater than that of man.

I was troubled. A mist came over my eyes, and I felt faint. But I was quickly restored by the cold wind of the mountains. As the shape came nearer, I saw a sight both tremendous and hated! It was the wretch whom I had created. I trembled with rage and horror. I decided to wait for his approach and then engage in mortal combat with him.

He approached. His face showed bitter suffering,

combined with scorn and hate. Its unearthly ugliness made it almost too horrible for human eyes. But I hardly noticed this. Rage and hatred had at first made me unable to speak. I recovered, only to overwhelm him with words of furious hatred.

"Devil," I exclaimed. "Do you dare approach me? Don't you fear the fierce **vengeance** of my arm leashed on your miserable head? Go away, horrid insect! Or rather, stay, so that I may trample you to dust! And, oh! If I could destroy your miserable life! But that wouldn't restore those victims whom you have so wickedly murdered!"

"I expected this reaction from you," said the demon. "All men hate those who are offensive to them. How, then, must I be hated. I am miserable beyond all living things!

"Yet you, my creator, scorn and **spurn** me, your creature. You and I are bound by the strongest ties. And those ties can only be broken by the death of one of us.

"You mean to kill me," he continued. "How dare you play thus with life? Do your duty towards me. Then I will do mine towards you and the rest of mankind. If you agree to my conditions, I will leave them and you at peace.

"But if you refuse, I will flood the jaws of death. I will flood them until they are satisfied with the blood of your remaining friends."

"Hated monster!" I cried. "Fiend that you are! The tortures of hell are too mild a vengeance for your crimes. Wretched devil! You find fault with me for creating you. Come on, then. Let me put out the spark which I so wrongfully gave."

My rage knew no bounds, and I sprang on him. I was driven by all the feelings which can arm one man against another. But he easily escaped me.

"Be calm!" he said. "I beg you to hear me. Don't bring down your hatred on my devoted head. Haven't I suffered enough, without you seeking to increase my

misery? Life may only be suffering upon suffering. But
life is dear to me, and I will defend it.

"Remember, you have made me more powerful than
yourself. My height is greater than yours, my joints more
flexible. But I won't be tempted to set myself against you.
"I am your creature," he continued. "I will be even
mild and obedient to my natural lord and king. But you
will also perform your part. You owe it to me. Oh,
Frankenstein, don't be fair to every other man and then
trample upon me alone. To me, your justice—and even
your mercy and affection—is most due.

"Remember that I am your creature. I ought to be
your Adam, but instead I am the fallen angel.[5] You have
driven me from joy for no reason. I see happiness
everywhere, yet I am completely left out. I was kindly
and good. Misery made me a fiend. Make me happy, and
I shall again be good and decent."

"Go!" I cried. "I won't listen to you. There can be no
friendship between you and me. We are enemies. Leave
me alone, or let us try our strength in a fight. One of us
must fall."

"How can I get through to you?" asked the demon.
"Will no words cause you to turn a kind eye upon your
creature? I beg for your goodness and compassion.
Believe me, Frankenstein, I was kind. My soul glowed
with love and kindness.

"But am I not alone, miserably alone? You, my
creator, hate me. What hope can I gather from your
fellow creatures? They don't owe me anything. They
spurn and hate me.

"The desert mountains and dreary glaciers are my
hiding place," the monster went on. "I have wandered
here many days. I alone do not fear the caves of ice. They
are a home to me, and the only one which I am allowed. I
greet the bleak skies. They are kinder to me than your

---

[5] The fallen angel refers to Satan. It will eventually be revealed that the
monster has read *Paradise Lost* by John Milton (1608-1674). This epic poem
includes a description of Satan being thrust out of heaven.

fellow beings.

"If most of mankind knew I existed, they would do as you do. They would try to destroy me. Shouldn't I then hate those who hate me? I'll make no agreements with my enemies. I am miserable, and they shall share my misery.

"Yet it is in your power to make peace with me," the demon went on. "You can deliver mankind from a terrible evil. Otherwise, you will make this evil so great that you and your family shall be swallowed up in the whirlwinds of its rage. Then thousands of others shall follow.

"Let your compassion be moved, and don't **despise** me. Listen to my tale. When you have heard that, abandon me or befriend me. You shall judge which I deserve. But hear me. The guilty are allowed this much by human laws, bloody as they are. They can speak in their own defense before they are condemned.

"Listen to me, Frankenstein. You accuse me of murder. And yet you would destroy your own creature with a satisfied conscience. Oh, praise the eternal justice of man! Yet I don't ask you to spare me. Listen to me. Then, if you can, and if you will, destroy the work of your hands."

"Why do you bring back these memories?" I answered. "These are things which I shudder to think about. Things which I have been the miserable cause of. Cursed be the day in which you first saw light, hated devil! Cursed be the hands that formed you—although I curse myself!

"You have made me miserable beyond words," I went on. "You have left me no power to consider whether I am fair to you or not. Go! Relieve me from the sight of your hated form."

"Thus I relieve you, my creator," he said, and he placed his awful hands before my eyes. I flung them from me with violence. "Thus," he went on, "I take from you a sight which you can't stand. Still you can't listen to me and grant me your pity. By the goodness that I once possessed, I demand this from you.

"Hear my tale," continued the monster. "It is long and strange, and the weather here isn't fitting to your fine sensations. Come to the hut on the mountain.

"The sun is yet high in the heavens. It will soon hide itself behind your snowy peaks and light up another world. By then you will have heard my story and can decide.

"On you it rests whether I leave the neighborhood of man forever and lead a harmless life. Otherwise I shall become the ruin of your fellow creatures. And I shall be the cause of your own speedy ruin."

As he said this, he led the way across the ice. I followed. My heart was full, and I didn't answer him. But as I walked, I weighed the different arguments that he had used. I decided at least to listen to his tale. I was partly urged by curiosity, and pity settled my decision.

So far, I had supposed him to be the murderer of my brother. I eagerly sought a proof or denial of this opinion. For the first time, also, I felt what the duties of a creator towards his creature were. I knew I ought to make him happy before I complained of his wickedness.

These thoughts urged me to go along with his demand. Therefore, we crossed the ice and climbed the opposite rock. The air was cold, and the rain again began to come down.

We entered the hut, the fiend with an air of triumph. I myself had a heavy heart and depressed spirits. But I agreed to listen. I seated myself by the fire which my disagreeable companion had lighted. Thus, he began his tale.

Chapter 11

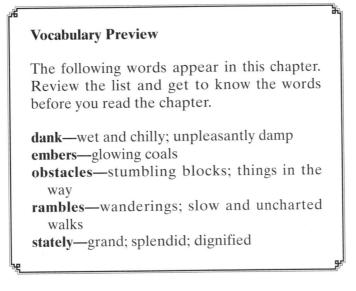

Vocabulary Preview

The following words appear in this chapter. Review the list and get to know the words before you read the chapter.

dank—wet and chilly; unpleasantly damp
embers—glowing coals
obstacles—stumbling blocks; things in the way
rambles—wanderings; slow and uncharted walks
stately—grand; splendid; dignified

[Note: The monster tells the story in Chapters 11-16.]

It is very hard to remember the time when I came to be. All the events of that period appear confused and unclear. A strange number of sensations came over me. I saw, felt, heard, and smelled at the same time.

"It was, indeed, a long time before I could tell my different senses apart. I remember a gradually stronger light pressed on my nerves. I was then forced to shut my eyes.

"Darkness then came over me and troubled me. But hardly had I felt this when—as I now suppose—I opened my eyes. Then the light poured in upon me again.

"I walked downwards, I believe. But I quickly found a great change in my sensations. Before, dark and shadowy bodies had surrounded me. They had been unknown to my touch or sight. But I now found that I could wander on at liberty. I met no **obstacles** that I couldn't either overcome or avoid.

"The light became more and more unpleasant to me, and the heat tired me as I walked. So I looked for some shade. I found it in the forest near Ingolstadt. Here I lay by the side of a brook. I rested from my exhaustion until I felt tormented by hunger and thirst.

"This roused me from my almost sleeping state. I then ate some berries that I found hanging on the trees or lying on the ground. I quenched my thirst at the brook. Then I lay down and was overcome by sleep. It was dark when I awoke. I felt cold also, and half frightened, naturally, finding myself so alone.

"Before I had left your apartment, I felt cold. So I had covered myself with some clothes. But these weren't enough to protect me from the chill of night.

"I was a poor, helpless, miserable wretch. I neither knew nor recognized anything. But when I felt pain invade me on all sides, I sat down and wept.

"Soon a gentle light stole over the heavens, giving me a sensation of pleasure. I stood up and watched a radiant form rise from among the trees. Later I discovered it was the moon. I gazed with a kind of wonder. It moved slowly, but it lighted my path, and I again went out in search of berries.

"I was still cold when I found a huge cloak under one of the trees. I covered myself with it and sat down on the ground.

"No clear ideas filled my mind. Everything was so confusing. I felt light, and hunger, and thirst, and darkness. Countless sounds rang in my ears. On all sides different scents greeted me. The only object that I could make out was the bright moon. I fixed my eyes on that with pleasure.

"Several changes of day and night passed. The sphere of the moon had greatly lessened. I began to tell my senses from each other. I gradually saw plainly the clear stream that supplied me with drink. I also saw the trees that shaded me with their leaves.

"A certain pleasant sound had often greeted my ears.

I was delighted when I first discovered that it came from the throats of little winged animals. These animals had often come between my eyes and the light. "I began also to better observe the forms that surrounded me. I saw the boundaries of the radiant roof of light that hung over me.

"Sometimes I tried to copy the pleasant songs of the birds but was unable. Sometimes I wished to express my sensations in my own way. But rude and meaningless sounds broke from me. They frightened me into silence again.

"The moon had disappeared from the night while I still remained in the forest. Then it showed itself again with a lessened form. By this time, my senses had become clearly separate from one another. My mind received new ideas every day.

"My eyes became used to the light and I began to see objects in their right forms. I could tell the insect from the herb. Then, gradually, I could tell one herb from another. I found that the sparrow uttered only unpleasant notes. But the sounds of the blackbird and thrush were sweet and pleasing.

"One day, when I was suffering from the cold, I found a fire. It apparently had been left by some wandering beggars. I was overcome with delight at the warmth that came from it.

"In my joy I thrust my hand into the live **embers.** But I quickly drew it out again with a cry of pain. How strange, I thought, that the same cause should produce such opposite effects!

"I examined the materials of the fire. To my joy I found it to be composed of wood. I quickly collected some branches, but they were wet and wouldn't burn. I was unhappy about this and sat still watching the workings of the fire. The wet wood which I had placed near the heat dried. Then it, too, became inflamed.

"I thought this over. By touching the various branches, I discovered the cause. Then I busied myself in collecting a large amount of wood. I could dry it and have a plentiful supply of fire.

"Then night came on and brought sleep with it. I was in the greatest fear that my fire would go out. I covered it carefully with dry wood and leaves and placed wet branches on it. Then, spreading my cloak, I lay on the ground and sank into sleep.

"It was morning when I awoke. My first care was to visit the fire. I uncovered it, and a gentle breeze quickly fanned it into a flame. I observed this also and invented a fan of branches. This roused the embers when they were nearly put out.

"When night came again, I found with pleasure that the fire gave light as well as heat. I also found out that fire was useful to me in my food. For I found some of the scraps that the travelers had left which had been roasted. They tasted much more pleasant than the berries I gathered from the trees.

"Therefore, I tried to prepare my food in the same manner. I placed it on the live embers. I found that the berries were spoiled by this operation. But the nuts and roots were much improved.

"However, food became scarce. I often spent the whole day searching in vain for a few acorns to ease my hunger pangs. As a result, I decided to leave the place where I had so far been living. I went to look for one where the few needs I had would be more easily satisfied.

"In this move, I greatly mourned the loss of the fire. I had gotten it through accident and didn't know how to make another one. I spent several hours considering this difficulty. But I was forced to give up on it.

"So I wrapped myself up in my cloak and struck across the wood towards the setting sun. I spent three days on these **rambles.** At length, I discovered the open country.

"A great snowfall had taken place the night before. The fields were of one solid whiteness. The appearance was terribly lonely. I found my feet chilled by the cold, damp substance that covered the ground.

"It was about seven in the morning, and I longed to find food and shelter. At last I spotted a small hut on a little hill. It had doubtless been built for the convenience of some shepherd. This was a new sight to me, and I examined the building with great curiosity.

"Finding the door open, I entered. An old man sat inside, near a fire. He was preparing his breakfast. He turned on hearing a noise. Seeing me, he shrieked loudly and fled the hut. He ran across the fields with a speed which his lame form hardly appeared capable of.

"His appearance was different from any I had ever seen before. And his flight somewhat surprised me. But I was enchanted by the appearance of the hut.

"Inside, the snow and rain couldn't come through, and the ground was dry. The place seemed to me a perfect, safe place. It appeared much as Pandemonium appeared to the demons of hell after their sufferings in the lake of fire.[1]

"I greedily ate what was left of the shepherd's breakfast—some bread, cheese, milk, and wine. The wine, however, I didn't like. Then, overcome by tiredness, I lay down among some straw and fell asleep.

"It was noon when I awoke. I was charmed by the warmth of the sun, which shone brightly on the white ground. I decided to begin my travels. I put the remains of the peasant's breakfast in a small bag I found. Then I walked across the fields for several hours. At sunset, I at last arrived at a village.

"How miraculous this appeared! The huts, the neater cottages, and **stately** houses all inspired my admiration. There were vegetables in the gardens. I saw milk and cheese placed at the windows of some of the cottages. I felt hungry.

"I entered one of the best of the cottages. But I had hardly placed my foot within the door before the children

---

[1] In the epic poem *Paradise Lost*, Pandemonium is a great city in Hell where demons take refuge after being cast into a lake of fire.

screamed and one of the women fainted. The whole village was roused. Some fled, some attacked me. I was horribly bruised by stones and many other kinds of missile weapons.

"At last, I escaped to the open country and fearfully took refuge in a tiny shack. It was quite bare and seemed miserable after the palaces I had seen in the village. However, this shack was attached to a cottage with a neat and pleasant appearance. But after my recent, dearly earned lesson, I didn't dare enter it.

"My place of refuge was made of wood, but it was so low that I could only sit up in it with difficulty. No wood was placed on the earth, which formed the floor, but it was dry. And although the wind entered it by countless openings, I found it an agreeably safe place from the snow and rain.

"Here, then, I retreated and lay down. I was happy to have found a shelter, however miserable, from the harshness of the season. Still more, I was protected from the cruelty of man.

"As soon as morning dawned I crept from my shelter. I wanted to view the attached cottage. I needed to know if I could remain in the shelter I had found.

"The shack was placed against the back of the cottage, and its visible sides were surrounded by a pig sty and a clear pool of water. One part was open, and that was where I had crept in.

"With stones and wood I covered every opening through which I might be seen by someone. I did it in such a way that I could move them when I wanted to go out. All the light I enjoyed came through the sty, and that was enough for me.

"Thus I arranged my dwelling and carpeted it with clean straw. Then I went inside, for I saw the figure of a man at a distance. I remembered my treatment the night before too well to risk being seen by anyone.

"I had first provided for my food that day, however. This was a loaf of coarse bread, which I stole. I also took a cup, from which I could drink more easily the pure water which flowed by my shack. The floor was a little raised, so it was kept perfectly dry. And because of its nearness to the chimney of the cottage, it was warm enough.

"So I had thus provided for myself. Now I decided to live in this shack until something should occur which might change my mind. It was indeed a paradise compared to the dreary forest. I remembered the rain-dropping branches and dank earth.

"I ate my breakfast with pleasure and was about to remove a board to get myself a little water. But then I heard a step. Looking through a small opening, I saw a young creature. She held a pail on her head as she passed before my shack.

"The girl was young and wore a gentle expression. She wasn't like a normal cottager or farmhouse servant. Yet she was poorly dressed. A rough blue petticoat[2] and a linen jacket were her only clothes. And her fair hair was braided but wore no ornaments. She looked patient, yet sad.

"I lost sight of her. But in about a quarter of an hour she returned bearing the pail, which was now partly filled with milk. She walked along, not seeming to notice her burden.

"Then a young man met her. His face showed a deeper sadness, and he uttered a few gloomy sounds. He took the pail from her head and carried it to the cottage himself. She followed, and they disappeared.

"Soon I saw the young man again with some tools in his hand. He crossed the field behind the cottage. The girl was also kept busy, sometimes in the house and sometimes in the yard.

"I examined my dwelling. I found that one of the windows of the cottage had once been a part of it. But the panes had been filled up with wood. In one of these was a

---

[2] A petticoat is a type of skirt worn by women.

small and almost invisible opening. The eye could just see through it.

"Through this hole I could see a small room. It was clean and painted white, but had little furniture. In one corner, near a small fire, sat an old man. He was leaning his head on his hands with an air of discouragement.

"The young girl was occupied in straightening up the cottage. But soon she took something out of a drawer which occupied her hands. Then she sat down beside the old man. He took up an instrument and began to play. The sounds he produced were sweeter than the voice of the birds.

"It was a lovely sight—even to me, poor wretch. I had never seen anything beautiful before. The silver hair and kindly face of the aged cottager won my respect. The gentle manners of the girl stirred my love.

"The old man played a sweet, mournful air. I saw that it drew tears from the eyes of his pleasant companion. The old man took no notice of this until she sobbed aloud. He then pronounced a few sounds. Then the fair creature left her work and knelt at his feet.

"He raised her and smiled with great kindness and affection. As I watched, strange feelings came over me. They were a mixture of pain and pleasure. It was like nothing I had ever before felt, either from hunger or cold, warmth or food. I went away from the window, unable to bear these emotions.

"Soon after this, the young man returned with a load of wood on his shoulders. The girl met him at the door and helped him with his burden. She took some of the fuel into the cottage and placed it on the fire.

"Then she and the youth went apart into a corner of the cottage. He showed her a large loaf and a piece of cheese. She seemed pleased and went into the garden for some roots and plants. She placed these in water, and then upon the fire.

"Afterwards she continued her work. In the meantime the young man went into the garden. There he worked at digging and pulling up roots.

"After he had dug and pulled for about an hour, the young woman joined him. They entered the cottage together. In the meantime, the old man had been thoughtful. But when his companions returned, he put on a more cheerful face. They sat down to eat.

"The meal was quickly gone. The young woman was again occupied in cleaning up the cottage. The old man walked outside in the sun for a few minutes, leaning on the arm of the young man.

"Nothing could be greater in beauty than the contrast between these two excellent creatures. One was old, with silver hairs and a face beaming with kindness and love. The other was slim and graceful in his figure. His features were molded in the finest shape. Yet his eyes and attitude showed the greatest sadness and gloom.

"The old man returned to the cottage. The youth took up different tools from those he had used in the morning. Then he went across the fields.

"Night quickly shut in. But to my extreme wonder, I found that the cottagers had a way of keeping the room light by the use of candles. So I was delighted to find that the setting of the sun didn't put an end to my pleasure. I could still watch my human neighbors.

"In the evening the young girl and her companion worked at their different chores. I didn't understand what they were doing. And the old man again took up the instrument. He produced the same divine sounds that had enchanted me in the morning.

"As soon as he was finished, the youth began to utter sounds, but he didn't play the instrument. His sounds were steady and flat. They weren't like the harmony of the old man's instrument nor the songs of the birds. I since found that he read aloud. But at that time I knew nothing of words or letters.

"The family occupied themselves thus for a short time. Then they put out their lights and retired, as I assumed, to rest."

Chapter 12 (Summary)

$\mathbf{A}$s the monster continued to observe the cottagers, he was struck by their great unhappiness. At first he could see no reason for this. But then he noticed that the cottagers seemed to be very poor. They barely had enough food to survive. When the monster realized this, he stopped stealing food from them. He went back to eating only berries, nuts, and roots.

Gradually, the monster began to learn by listening to the cottagers. He learned how humans express themselves through speech. One day he found out the names of the cottagers. The two young people were Agatha and Felix. The old man—who was blind—was called "Father." The monster also found out that humans could read and write.

But the monster also learned one horrifying fact. One day he happened to see his reflection in a pool of water. It was then that he realized why human beings ran from him in fear and disgust. However, he didn't know at the time how his horrid form would shape his future.

The goodness of the cottagers inspired the monster to help them. He secretly chopped wood during the night and left it at their door. The cottagers were astonished and pleased at this kindness. Later, the monster secretly did other chores for them, such as clearing snow from the path.

After a time the snow completely disappeared, and warmer weather took its place. But the cottagers were still unhappy. The monster grew more and more curious about the cottagers' sadness. He was determined to learn their story and maybe one day introduce himself to them. He dreamed of winning their love.

Meanwhile, with the arrival of spring, the monster's spirits improved. His awful past became a distant memory. He began thinking only of the peaceful present and a hopeful future.

Chapter 13 (Summary)

Spring quickly advanced. And with it came cloudless skies, warm weather, and wonderful, blooming growth. The monster's senses were refreshed by the scents and sights of beautiful flowers. For a while, things continued as normal in the cottage. Then a mysterious woman arrived on horseback. When Felix saw her, the stranger threw back her veil, revealing a beautiful and angelic young woman. Felix was overjoyed to see her. He introduced her to Agatha and his father as his "sweet Arabian." Felix's gloom left him now that this lovely woman had arrived.

The monster observed that the woman spoke differently from the cottagers. Indeed, she couldn't understand their speech, nor they hers. So Felix set about teaching her their language.[1] From his shack, the monster also took advantage of the lessons.

The monster learned that the woman's name was Safie. Every day, Felix taught her more and more words. And as the monster listened from his hut, he also benefitted from these lessons. In two months, he could understand the cottagers' language.

It seemed that sadness had been replaced by joy in the cottage. Safie and Agatha often sang and played the guitar. The old man was delighted by the sweet music.

Along with speech, Felix also taught Safie to read. The monster learned this skill as well. The book Felix used for his lessons dealt with human history and governments. The monster learned about both the good and evil sides of humankind. He learned that people had achieved noble things. But they also had committed terrible deeds against one another.

This new knowledge of humans puzzled the monster. How could people be so fine in some ways and so wicked

---

[1] The cottagers—and apparently the Frankensteins—speak French.

in others?

The monster also learned that the most respected people had both wealth and good looks. He was painfully aware that he had neither of these qualities. In fact, the more the monster learned about people, the more he felt like an outsider.

There seemed to be no one like him in the world. He remembered no childhood, no parents, no friends. Who was he? Where did he come from? And who was his creator? Over and over the monster asked himself these questions.

Chapter 14

Vocabulary Preview

The following words appear in this chapter.
Review the list and get to know the words
before you read the chapter.

banished—sent away; exiled
deceit—trickery; dishonesty
distinction—position; social class
fugitives—runaways; escapees
striving—trying; aiming
virtue—goodness; decency

Some time went by before I learned my friends' history.
Their story made a deep impression on my mind. I
learned a number of things, each interesting and
wonderful to one as inexperienced as I was.

"The old man's name was De Lacey. He came from a
good family in France, where he had lived in wealth for
many years. He had been respected by his superiors and
beloved by his equals. His son was raised in the service of
his country. And Agatha had ranked with ladies of the
highest **distinction.**

"A few months before my arrival they had lived in a
large and grand city called Paris. They were surrounded
by friends and had all sorts of enjoyments. They had
everything that **virtue** and education—combined with
reasonable wealth—could give them.

"Safie's father had been the cause of their ruin. He
was a Turkish merchant who had lived in Paris for many
years. Then, for some reason, he got into trouble with the
government. He was seized and cast into prison the very

day that Safie arrived from Constantinople[1] to join him. He was tried and sentenced to death.

"The injustice of his sentence was very obvious, and all Paris was enraged. People felt that the crime he was charged with wasn't the cause of his sentence. Rather, it was his religion and wealth.

"Felix had accidentally been present at the trial. His horror and anger were uncontrollable when he heard the court's decision. At that moment, he made a solemn vow to rescue the Turk. Then he looked around for a way to do it.

"Felix made many useless attempts to get into the prison. At last, he found a strongly grated window[2] in an unguarded part of the building. It lighted the dungeon of the unfortunate Muhammadan.[3] Loaded with chains, the Turk waited in despair for his sentence to be carried out.

"Felix visited the grate at night. He told the prisoner of his intentions. The Turk was amazed and delighted. He tried to stir up his rescuer's enthusiasm by promises of reward and wealth.

"Felix rejected the offers with scorn. But then he saw the lovely Safie, the Turk's daughter. She was allowed to visit her father. Her gestures expressed her lively gratitude to Felix, and the youth couldn't help thinking her a treasure. Surely, to gain Safie as his wife would fully reward his hard work and the danger he would put himself in.

"The Turk quickly noticed the impression that his daughter had made on Felix. He promised Felix Safie's hand in marriage. This promise would be fulfilled as soon as the Turk should be taken to a safe place.

"Felix was too much of a gentleman to accept this offer. Yet he looked forward to the likelihood of the event. It would make his happiness complete.

---

[1] Constantinople was the name of a city in Turkey. It is now called Istanbul.
[2] A grated window is covered by unbreakable bars to prevent people from getting through it.
[3] A Muhammadan is a follower of Muhammad (c. 570-632), the founder of the Islamic religion.

"During the following days, Felix worked on the merchant's escape. His enthusiasm was warmed by several letters that he received from this lovely girl. She was able to express her thoughts with the help of her father's servant, who understood French. She thanked him in the most passionate terms for what he intended to do for her father. At the same time, she gently complained of her own fate.

"I have copies of these letters. For during my stay in the shack I found a way to obtain writing tools. And the letters were often in the hands of Felix or Agatha. I'll give them to you before I leave. They will prove the truth of my tale. But at present, the sun is already near setting. I shall only have time to repeat the main elements of them to you.

"Safie explained that her mother was a Christian Arab. This woman had been seized and made a slave by the Turks. Highly regarded for her beauty, she won the heart of Safie's father, who married her.

"The young girl spoke in enthusiastic terms of her mother. Born in freedom, her mother rejected the bondage to which she was forced.

"She instructed her daughter in the teachings of her religion. She also taught her to reach for higher knowledge and an independence of spirit. These were forbidden to the female followers of Muhammad.

"This lady died, but Safie never forgot her lessons. She sickened at the thought of again returning to Asia. There she would be enclosed within the walls of a harem.⁴ And she would be allowed only to occupy herself with childish amusements.

"Such amusements were ill-suited to a girl of Safie's nature. She was too used to grand ideas and a noble **striving** for virtue. She preferred the possibility of marrying a Christian. Then she could remain in a country where women had some standing in society. The thought

---

⁴ A harem is where women live in a Muslim household.

was enchanting to her.

"The day for the Turk's death was set. But on the night before his execution, he fled his prison. Before morning he was many leagues away from Paris.

"Felix had obtained passports in the name of his father, sister, and himself. He had already told his father of his plan. Felix's father aided the **deceit** by pretending to set off on a journey. He then hid himself, with his daughter, in an out-of-the-way part of Paris.

"Felix led the **fugitives** through France to Lyons. They went across Mont Cenis to Leghorn.[5] There the Turk had decided to wait for a chance to move into some place under Turkish rule.

"Safie decided to remain with her father until the moment of his departure. Before that time, the Turk renewed his promise that she should be united to his rescuer. Felix remained with them, expecting that to happen.

"In the meantime Felix enjoyed the company of the Arabian woman. She showed him the simplest and tenderest affection. They were able to communicate with one another. Sometimes they used an interpreter; sometimes their looks alone were enough. And Safie sang to Felix the divine songs of her native country.

"The Turk allowed this friendship to take place and encouraged the hopes of the youthful lovers. But in his heart he had formed other plans far different.

"The Turk hated the idea of his daughter married to a Christian. But he feared Felix's resentment if he should appear lukewarm. For he knew that he was still in his rescuer's power. He didn't want Felix to betray him to the Italian state where they were staying.

"The Turk made a thousand plans by which he should be able to keep up the trick until it was no longer necessary. He secretly intended to take his daughter with

---

[5] Lyon (sometimes spelled *Lyons* in English) is the third largest city in France. Mont Cenis is east of Lyon, close to the French-Italian border. Leghorn is a city in northwest Italy.

him when he left. His plans were made possible by the news which arrived from Paris.

"The government of France was greatly enraged at the escape of their victim. They spared no pains to find and punish his rescuer. Felix's plot was quickly discovered, and Felix's father and Agatha were thrown into prison.

"The news reached Felix and roused him from his dream of pleasure. His blind and aged father and his gentle sister lay in a noisy dungeon. In the meantime, he enjoyed the free air and the society of the woman he loved. This idea was torture to him.

"He quickly made an arrangement with the Turk. Felix felt the latter might soon find a good opportunity for escape. If this happened before Felix could return to Italy, Safie should stay at a convent at Leghorn.

"Then, leaving the lovely Arabian, he hurried to Paris. There he gave himself up to the law. He hoped to free De Lacey and Agatha in this manner.

"He didn't succeed. They all remained in prison for five months before the trial took place. As a result of the trial, their fortune was taken away from them. And they were **banished** from their native country.

"They found a miserable shelter in the cottage in Germany, where I discovered them. Felix soon learned what the dishonest Turk—whom Felix and his family had suffered so much for—was up to.

"The Turk had discovered that his rescuer was reduced to poverty and ruin. He then became a traitor. He fled Italy with his daughter, insultingly sending Felix a small amount of money. He said it was to aid Felix in the future.

"Such were the events that weighed on Felix's heart. They made him the most miserable of his family when I first saw him.

"He could have endured poverty. Indeed, this distress brought out the best in him, and he gloried in it. But the ingratitude of the Turk and the loss of his beloved Safie were different. These misfortunes were more bitter and final. Thus the Arabian's arrival now gave new life to Felix's soul.

"When the news reached Leghorn of Felix's situation, the Turk commanded his daughter to think no more of her lover. Instead, she was to prepare to return to her native country.

"Safie was outraged by this order. She tried to reason with her father. But he left her angrily, stating again his cruel command.

"A few days later, the Turk entered his daughter's room. He hastily told her that he had reason to believe that his residence had been discovered. He might quickly be turned over to the French government. For this reason, he hired a boat to take him to Constantinople. He was going to sail for that city in a few hours.

"The Turk planned to leave his daughter under the care of a trusted servant. When she had a chance, she could follow him. She was to take with her most of his property, which hadn't yet arrived at Leghorn.

"When alone, Safie began to make a plan. She first considered what was the correct way to act in this emergency. The thought of living in Turkey was horrible to her. Her religion and her feelings both were against it.

"Then some of her father's papers fell into her hands. From them she learned of her lover's exile. She also learned the name of the spot where he then lived. She hesitated some time, but she finally formed her plan.

"She gathered together some jewels and money that belonged to her. Then she left Italy for Germany with a servant. This servant was a native of Leghorn, but she understood the common language of Turkey.

"Safie arrived in safety at a town about twenty leagues from De Lacey's cottage. Then her servant fell dangerously ill. Safie nursed her with the most devoted affection, but the poor girl died.

"The Arabian was left alone. She didn't know the language of the country. And she was unfamiliar with the ways of the world.

"However, Safie fell into good hands. Before her death, the servant had mentioned the name of the place where they were going. Afterwards, the woman of the house in which they had lived remembered this. She saw to it that Safie should safely arrive at her lover's cottage."

Chapter 15

Vocabulary Preview

The following words appear in this chapter. Review the list and get to know the words before you read the chapter.

bliss—great happiness; joy
despondency—depression; sadness
diligence—great effort; care
disdain—scorn; disgust
domestic—daily life; home
vices—faults; sins

Such was the history of my beloved cottagers. It impressed me deeply and formed my views of social life. From it I learned to admire their virtues and despise the **vices** of mankind.

"At this time, I looked upon crime as an evil far removed from me. Kindness and generosity were ever present before me. They filled me with a desire to become involved in the busy scene of life. I saw so many admirable qualities displayed before me.

"But in telling about the progress of my intelligence, there is one detail I must not leave out. It occurred in the beginning of the month of August of the same year.

"One night I made my usual visit to the neighboring wood. I began collecting my own food and gathering firewood for my protectors. While at work, I found on the ground a leather-covered trunk. It contained several pieces of clothing and some books.

"Fortunately, the books were written in the language which I had been learning little by little at the cottage.

They consisted of *Paradise Lost*, a volume of Plutarch's *Lives*, and *The Sorrows of Werther*.[1]

"Finding these treasures gave me extreme delight. I now continually studied and thought about these histories. In the meantime, my friends were busy with their usual activities.

"I can hardly describe to you what these books did for me. They produced in me countless new images and feelings. Sometimes they raised me to delight. But more often the books made me feel sad and hopeless.

"*The Sorrows of Werther* told a simple and touching story. It also contained many opinions and explained some things which had been strange to me. I found it a never-ending source of wonder and astonishment.

"The book described a gentle and simple life. But it also dealt with deeper feelings. These ideas were similar to my experience among my protectors and my own emotions.

"I thought Werther himself a more divine being than I had ever seen or imagined. His character was deep and honest. The discussions of death and suicide filled me with wonder.

"I didn't pretend to understand the rights and wrongs of Werther's actions. But I leaned towards the opinions of the hero. I wept at his death without really understanding it.

"However, as I read, I compared much to my own feelings and condition. I found myself similar to the beings I read about and whose conversations I listened to. And yet at the same time I was strangely unlike them.

"I sympathized with and partly understood them. But my mind was still unformed. I was dependent on no one and related to no one. 'The path of my departure was free,' and there was no one to mourn my doom.

---

[1] Plutarch (A.D. c. 46-c. 120) was a Greek biographer whose *Parallel Lives* tells the stories of important Greeks and Romans. *The Sorrows of Young Werther* is a novel by Johann Wolfgang von Goethe (1749-1832) in which a sensitive young hero commits suicide.

"My person was ugly and my build gigantic. What did this mean? Who was I? What was I? From where did I come? Where was I going? These questions continually returned to me. But I couldn't solve them.

"The volume of Plutarch's *Lives* which I found contained the histories of the first founders of the ancient republics.[2] This book had a much different effect on me from *The Sorrows of Werther*. I learned misery and gloom from Werther. But Plutarch taught me high thoughts. He raised me above my own miserable reflections. He taught me to admire and love the ancient heroes.

"I couldn't understand many of the things I read. I had a very confused knowledge of kingdoms, wide ranges of country, mighty rivers, and great seas. But I knew nothing of towns and large groups of people.

"The cottage of my protectors had been the only school in which I had studied human nature. But this book showed me new and mightier scenes of action. I read of men involved with public affairs, governing or destroying other men. I felt a great desire for virtue rise within me. And I felt a hatred for evil. These terms were difficult, and I didn't fully understand their meanings. So I could apply them only to pleasure and pain.

"Urged on by these feelings, I began to admire peaceable lawgivers. These included Numa, Solon, and Lycurgus, but not Romulus and Theseus.[3]

"The kindly lives of my protectors led me to feel the way I did. Perhaps it would have been different if my first view of humanity had been a young soldier, burning for glory and slaughter. Then I should have been charged with different feelings.

"But *Paradise Lost* excited different and far deeper

---

[2] A republic is a government ruled by the people or their representatives instead of a king or dictator.

[3] Romulus was the legendary founder of Rome. Numa became ruler of Rome after Romulus. Solon was an Athenian poet, leader, and social reformer during the early 6th century B.C. Lycurgus helped to found the Greek city-state of Sparta during the 9th century B.C. Theseus was a legendary Greek hero and ruler.

emotions. I read it as a true history, as I had read the other volumes which had fallen into my hands.

"It portrayed an all-powerful God at war with his creatures. And it moved every feeling of wonder and awe in me. I often compared its several situations to my own, as their similarity struck me. "Like Adam, I seemed to be connected by no link to any other living being. But his state was far different from mine in every other respect. He had come forth from the hands of God as a perfect creature. He was happy and had everything he needed. He was carefully guarded by his Creator. And he was allowed to speak with and learn from greater beings. But I was miserable, helpless, and alone.

"Many times I considered Satan as the fitter image of my condition. For often—like him—I viewed the **bliss** of my protectors, and a bitter taste of envy rose within me.

"Something else strengthened and confirmed these feelings. Soon after my arrival in the shack, I discovered some papers. These had been in the pocket of the clothes which I had taken from your laboratory. At first I had ignored them. But now I was able to read the words. So I began to study them with **diligence.**

"It was your journal of the four months that came before my creation. You carefully described in these papers every step you took in the progress of your work. This history was mixed with accounts of **domestic** happenings.

"You doubtless remember these papers. Here they are. Everything is told in them which has anything to do with my cursed beginning.

"Every detail of that series of disgusting circumstances which produced me is set in view. The smallest description of my foul and hateful person is given. Your language painted your own horrors and made mine unforgettable. I was sick as I read it.

" 'Hateful day when I received life!' I exclaimed in agony. 'Devilish creator! Why did you form a monster so horrible and ugly that even *you* turned from me in disgust?

" 'God, in pity, made man beautiful and attractive, after his own image. But my form is a filthy imitation of yours. It's even more horrid because of the likeness. Satan had his companions—fellow devils—to admire and encourage him. But I am alone and hated.'

"These were my thoughts during the hours of **despondency** and being alone. But then I considered the virtues of the cottagers. They were friendly and kindly by nature. I convinced myself that they would care for me when they learned how much I admired them. They would overlook my personal ugliness.

"Could they turn me from their door? Monstrous as I was, I only wanted their compassion and friendship. I decided at least not to despair. In every way I must prepare for a meeting with them that would decide my fate.

"I put off this attempt for some months longer. The importance of its success filled me with dread. What if I should fail? Besides, I found that I learned new things every day. Thus I was unwilling to begin this undertaking for a while. During that time I could add greatly to my knowledge.

"In the meantime, several changes took place in the cottage. Safie's presence spread happiness among the occupants. I also found they were no longer as poor as they had been. Felix and Agatha spent more time in amusement and conversation. They were now aided in their work by servants.

"They didn't appear rich, but they were contented and happy. Their feelings were calm and peaceful, while mine became more disturbed every day. More knowledge only showed to me more clearly what a wretched outcast I was.

"I cherished hope, it's true. But that hope left me when I looked at my person reflected in the water or my shadow in the moonshine. It didn't matter that my reflection was frail or my shadow unfaithful.

"I tried hard to crush these fears. I had to strengthen myself for the trial which I decided to undergo in a few months.

"Sometimes I allowed my thoughts—unstopped by reason—to ramble in the fields of Paradise. I dared to imagine pleasant and lovely creatures sympathizing with my feelings and cheering my gloom. I saw their angelic faces breathe smiles of comfort. But it was all a dream. No Eve soothed my sorrows nor shared my thoughts. I was alone.

"I remembered Adam's appeal to his Creator. But where was my creator? He had abandoned me, and in the bitterness of my heart I cursed him.

"Autumn passed in this way. With surprise and grief, I saw the leaves decay and fall. Nature again took on the barren and bleak appearance it had worn when I first saw the woods and the lovely moon.

"Yet I paid no attention to the dreary weather. My body was better able to endure cold rather than heat. But my biggest delights were the sights of the flowers, the birds, and all the bright clothing of summer. When those were gone, I turned with more attention towards the cottagers.

"The absence of summer didn't lessen their happiness. They loved and sympathized with one another. Their joys depended on each other and weren't interrupted by the change in the weather.

"The more I saw of them, the greater my desire became to gain their protection and kindness. My heart longed to be known and loved by these good-hearted creatures. I wanted to see their sweet looks directed towards me with affection. This was my greatest desire.

"I dared not think that they would turn from me with **disdain** and horror. The poor who stopped at their door were never driven away. It's true that I asked for greater treasures than a little food or rest. I required kindness and sympathy. But I didn't believe I was completely unworthy of it.

"The winter came. All of the seasons had taken place since I awoke to life. My attention now became focused on one thing—how to introduce myself to my protectors. "I thought over many plans. But the one I finally decided on was to enter the cottage when the blind old man was alone. I was intelligent enough to accept my unnatural ugliness. I knew it was the biggest object of horror with those who had seen me before.

"My voice was harsh but had nothing terrible in it. Therefore, I decided to wait for the absence of the blind man's children. Then I could gain the trust and good will of the old De Lacey. In this way, I might be accepted by my younger protectors.

"One day, the sun shone on the red leaves that were scattered upon the ground. It spread cheerfulness, although it gave no warmth. Safie, Agatha, and Felix left on a long country walk. The old man, by his own wish, was left alone in the cottage.

"When his children had gone, he took up his guitar. He played several mournful but sweet songs. They were more sweet and mournful than I had ever heard him play before.

"At first, his face was lit up with pleasure. But as he continued, thoughtfulness and sadness came over him. At last, he lay aside his instrument and sat caught up in his memories.

"My heart beat quick. This was the hour and moment which would decide my hopes or realize my fears. The servants were gone to a neighboring fair. All was silent in and around the cottage. It was an excellent opportunity. Yet, when I started to carry out my plan, my limbs failed me. I sank to the ground.

"I rose again with a firm purpose. I removed the planks I had placed before my shack to conceal my hiding place. The fresh air revived me. With renewed determination, I walked to the door of the cottage.

"I knocked. 'Who is there?' said the old man. 'Come in.'

"I entered. 'Pardon me,' I said. 'I'm a traveler in need of a little rest. May I sit before the fire for a few minutes?'

" 'Enter,' said De Lacey. 'I will do what I can to relieve your needs. But unfortunately, my children are away. And as I'm blind, I'm afraid I shall find it difficult to get food for you.'

" 'Do not trouble yourself, my kind host. I have food. It is only warmth and rest that I need.'

"I sat down, and a silence fell. I knew that every minute was precious to me. Yet I couldn't decide how to begin the interview. Then the old man spoke.

" 'By your language, stranger, I suppose you are my countryman,' he said. 'Are you French?'

" 'No,' said I. 'But I was educated by a French family and understand that language only. I'm now going to claim the protection of some friends whom I sincerely love. I have some hopes that they will welcome me.'

" 'Are they Germans?' asked the old man.

" 'No, they are French,' I said. 'But let us change the subject. I am an unfortunate and deserted creature. I look around and I have no relative or friend on earth. These kind people I am going to have never seen me before. They know little of me. I am full of fears. For if I fail there, I'm an outcast in the world forever.'

" 'Do not despair,' said the old man. 'To be friendless is indeed unfortunate. But the hearts of men are not always selfish. They are often full of brotherly love and charity. Therefore, depend on your hopes. If these friends are good and kind, do not despair.'

" 'They are kind,' said I. 'They are the most excellent creatures in the world. But unfortunately, they are prejudiced against me. I am good by nature. My life has so far been harmless. It has even been of some good, to a certain degree. But a fatal prejudice clouds their eyes. They ought to see a good-hearted and kind friend, but they see only a hateful monster.'

" 'That is indeed unfortunate,' said the old man. 'But

if you are really blameless, can't you make them see the truth?'

" 'I am about to try,' said I. 'It is for that reason that I feel so many overwhelming terrors. I tenderly love these friends. I have—unknown to them—been doing kind acts towards them for many months. But they believe that I wish to injure them. It is that prejudice that I wish to overcome.'

" 'Where do these friends live?' asked the old man.

" 'Near this spot.' said I.

"The old man paused and then continued. 'Tell me every detail of your story. Then perhaps I may be of use in telling them the truth.

" 'I'm blind and can't judge you by your face,' he went on. 'But there is something in your words that tells me that you're sincere. I am poor and an exile. But it will give me true pleasure to be helpful to a human creature in any way.'

" 'Excellent man!' said I. 'I thank you and accept your generous offer. You raise me from the dust by this kindness. I trust that, with your help, I shall not be driven from the society and sympathy of your fellow creatures.'

" 'Heaven forbid!' said the old man. 'Even if you were a criminal, you should not be driven away. That would only drive you to desperation and not bring you to virtue. I also am unfortunate. I and my family have been condemned, although innocent. So decide for yourself if I do not feel for your misfortunes.'

" 'How can I thank you, my best and only friend?' said I. 'It is from your lips that I have first heard a kind voice directed towards me. I shall be forever grateful. And your compassion assures me of success with my friends.'

" 'May I know the names and home of those friends?' asked the old man.

"I paused. This, I thought, was the moment of decision. It would rob me of happiness or bring it to me forever. I struggled in vain for the courage to answer him.

But the effort destroyed all my remaining strength. I sank on the chair and sobbed aloud.

"At that moment, I heard the steps of my younger protectors. I didn't have a moment to lose. I grabbed the old man's hand.

" 'Now is the time!' I cried. 'Save and protect me! You and your family are the friends whom I seek. Don't desert me in the hour of trial!'

" 'Great God!' exclaimed the old man. 'Who are you?'

"At that instant the cottage door was opened. Felix, Safie, and Agatha entered. Who can describe their horror and amazement on seeing me? Agatha fainted. Safie, unable to help her friend, rushed out of the cottage.

"Felix darted forward. With supernatural force he tore me from his father, to whose knees I clung. In a surge of fury, he dashed me to the ground and struck me violently with a stick. I could have torn him limb from limb, as the lion tears the antelope. But my heart sank within me as if I were sick, and I held back.

"I saw him about to repeat his blow. Overcome by pain and suffering, I fled the cottage. In the general confusion, I escaped unseen to my shack."

Chapter 16

Vocabulary Preview

The following words appear in this chapter. Review the list and get to know the words before you read the chapter.

atone—make up for; pay the penalty
exquisite—fine; excellent
havoc—great damage; ruin
invulnerable—not able to be hurt or destroyed; unconquerable
novelty—newness; strangeness
ogre—monster

Cursed, cursed creator! Why did I live? Why didn't I instantly put out the spark of life which you so shamefully gave? I don't know.

"Despair hadn't yet taken hold of me. My feelings were those of rage and revenge. I could have destroyed the cottage and the people in it with pleasure. I would have delighted in their shrieks and misery.

"When night came, I fled my shack and wandered the wood. I was no longer held back by the fear of discovery. So I gave vent to my agony in fearful howlings. I was like a wild beast that had been freed. I destroyed the objects that stood in my way and wandered through the wood with a staglike swiftness.

"Oh! What a miserable night I passed! The cold stars shone in mockery. The bare trees waved their branches above me. Now and then the sweet voice of a bird burst forth amidst the stillness.

"All except I were resting or enjoying themselves.

Like the devil, I had a hell within me. No one sympathized with me. I wished to tear up the trees and spread **havoc** and destruction around me. Afterwards I could sit down and enjoy the ruin.

"But this feeling was a luxury that I couldn't keep up. I became exhausted from bodily exercise. On the damp grass, I sank in the sick helplessness of despair.

"There was no one in the world who would pity me or help me. Should I then feel kindness towards my enemies? No. From that moment I declared everlasting war against man. I especially hated the one who had formed me and sent me forth to this unbearable misery.

"The sun rose. I heard men's voices and knew that it was impossible to return to my shelter during that day. Therefore, I hid myself in some thick underwood. I decided to spend the coming hours thinking about my situation.

"The pleasant sunshine and the pure air of day brought back my calmness somewhat. I thought over what had happened at the cottage. I couldn't help believing that I had been too quick in my judgment.

"I had certainly acted unwisely. It was apparent that my conversation had swayed the father on my behalf. I was a fool in having shown myself to the horror of his children.

"I ought to have let the old De Lacey get to know me. Then gradually the rest of his family would have been prepared to see me.

"But I didn't believe my errors were unfixable. After much thought, I decided to return to the cottage. I would seek the old man. I would explain things to him and win him to my side.

"These thoughts calmed me, and in the afternoon I sank into a deep sleep. But I was still too disturbed to have peaceful dreams. The horrible scene of the day before was forever happening before my eyes. The females were flying, and the enraged Felix was tearing me from his father's feet.

"I awoke exhausted. I found that it was already night, so I crept from my hiding place and went to look for food.

"When my hunger was eased, I turned toward the well-known path that led to the cottage. All there was at peace. I crept into my shack and remained there. Silently I awaited the usual hour when the family arose.

"That hour passed, and the sun rose high in the heavens. But the cottagers didn't appear. I trembled violently, expecting some dreadful misfortune. The inside of the cottage was dark, and I heard no motion. I can't describe the agony of this suspense.

"Soon two countrymen passed by. Pausing near the cottage, they entered into conversation, using violent gestures. I didn't understand what they said. They spoke the language of the country, which differed from that of my protectors.

"However, Felix approached soon after with another man. I was surprised, as I knew that he hadn't left the cottage that morning. I waited anxiously to discover from his words what was going on.

" 'Haven't you considered,' his companion said to him, 'that you will have to pay three months' rent? You will also lose what you have grown in your garden. I don't wish to take any unfair advantage. Therefore, I beg you to take some days to consider your decision.'

" 'It is completely useless,' replied Felix. 'We can never again live in your cottage. My father's life is in the greatest danger. I have already told you the dreadful circumstances. My wife and my sister will never recover from their horror. I beg you not to reason with me any more. Take possession of your miserable house and let me leave this place.'

"Felix trembled violently as he said this. He and his companion entered the cottage. They remained there for a few moments and then left. I never saw any of the De Lacey family again.

"I spent the remainder of the day in my shack. I was in a state of total and numb despair. My protectors had

gone. The only link that held me to the world was broken.
"For the first time the feelings of revenge and hatred
filled my bosom. I didn't try to control them. I allowed
myself to be borne away by the stream. I bent my mind
towards injury and death.

"I thought of my friends, of the mild voice of De Lacey,
the gentle eyes of Agatha, and the **exquisite** beauty of the
Arabian. Then these thoughts vanished and a gush of tears
somewhat soothed me.

"But again I remembered that they had rejected and
deserted me. My anger returned—a rage of anger.
Unable to injure anything human, I turned my fury
towards lifeless objects.

"As night advanced, I placed a variety of burnable
objects around the cottage. I destroyed every growing
thing in the garden. Then I waited with great impatience
until the moon had sunk to begin my activities.

"The night came. A fierce wind arose from the
woods. It quickly spread the clouds that had hung in the
heavens. The blast tore along like a mighty avalanche. It
produced a kind of madness in me that went beyond all
reason and thought.

"I lighted the dry branch of a tree and danced with
fury around the cottage. I kept my eyes fixed on the
western horizon, which the edge of the moon nearly
touched. A part of the moon was finally hid, and I waved
my torch. It sank, and with a loud scream I fired the
straw, twigs, and bushes which I had collected.

"The wind fanned the fire. The cottage was quickly
surrounded by the flames. They clung to the little
building and licked it with their forked and destroying
tongues.

"Soon I was convinced that nothing could save any
part of the home. I left the scene and sought for safety in
the woods.

"And now, with the world before me, where should I
go? I decided to fly far from the scene of my misfortunes.
But to me, hated and despised, every country must be

equally horrible.

"At last, the thought of you crossed my mind. I learned from your papers that you were my father, my creator. And who better could I go to than to the one who had given me life?

"Among the lessons that Felix had given to Safie, geography hadn't been left out. I had learned from these the basic locations of the different countries of the earth. You had mentioned Geneva as the name of your native town. Towards this place I decided to go.

"But how was I to find the way? I knew that I must travel in a southwesterly direction to reach my destination. But the sun was my only guide. I didn't know the names of the towns I was to pass through. Nor could I ask information from a single human being.

"But I didn't despair. Only from you could I hope for comfort, though all I felt toward you was hatred. Unfeeling, heartless creator! You had given me feelings and passions. Then you cast me out, an object for the scorn and horror of mankind.

"But only on you did I have any claim for pity and repayment. I had tried in vain to gain justice from any other human being. Now I decided to seek it from you.

"My travels were long and I suffered greatly. It was late in autumn when I left the district where I had lived for so long. I traveled only at night, afraid of meeting the face of a human being.

"Nature decayed around me, and the sun became heatless. Rain and snow poured around me, and mighty rivers were frozen. The surface of the earth was hard and chill and bare. I could find no shelter.

"Oh, earth! How often did I scream curses on the cause of my being! The mildness of my nature had fled. All within me was turned to hate and bitterness.

"The nearer I approached to your home, the more deeply I felt the spirit of revenge inflame in my heart. Snow fell, and the waters were hardened, but I didn't rest.

"A few incidents now and then directed me on my

way, and I had a map of the country. But I often
wandered wide from my path. The agony of my feelings
allowed me no rest. No incident occurred to lessen my
rage and misery.

"At last, I arrived at the border of Switzerland. The
sun had just then recovered its warmth, and the earth
again began to look green.

"Then something happened. It caused me to become
even more hardened in the bitterness and horror of my
feelings.

"I generally rested during the day. I traveled only
when I was hidden by night from the view of man.
However, one morning I found that my path lay through
a deep wood. So I decided to continue my journey after
the sun had risen.

"The day was one of the first of spring. The lovely
sunshine and mild air cheered even me. I felt emotions of
gentleness and pleasure. These feelings had long
appeared dead, but now they revived within me.

"I was half-surprised by the **novelty** of these
sensations. But I allowed myself to be carried away by
them. I forgot my loneliness and ugliness and dared to be
happy. Soft tears again dampened my cheeks. I even
raised my moist eyes with thankfulness towards the
blessed sun, which gave me such joy.

"I continued to follow the paths of the wood until I
came to its edge. There I caught sight of a deep and rapid
river. Many trees—budding with the fresh spring—bent
their branches into it.

"Here I paused, not exactly knowing what path to
take. Then I heard the sound of voices. I concealed
myself under the shade of a cypress tree.

"I was scarcely hid when a young girl came running
towards the spot where I was. She was laughing, as if she
ran from someone in fun. She continued her course along
the steep sides of the river. Suddenly her foot slipped, and
she fell into the rapid stream.

"I rushed from my hiding place. With great difficulty I

saved her from the force of the water and dragged her to the shore. She was unconscious, and I tried by every means in my power to restore life to her.

"But I was suddenly interrupted by the approach of a farmer. He was probably the person from whom she had playfully fled. On seeing me, he darted towards me and tore the girl from my arms. Then he hurried towards the deeper parts of the wood.

"I followed quickly—I hardly knew why. But then the man saw me draw near. He took a gun which he carried, aimed at my body, and fired. I sank to the ground. The man escaped into the wood with increased swiftness.

"This then was the reward for my kindness! I had saved a human being from death. As payment, I now squirmed under the miserable pain of a gunshot wound which shattered the flesh and bone.

"A few moments before, I had held feelings of kindness and gentleness. But now these gave place to hellish rage and gnashing of teeth. Inflamed by pain, I vowed eternal hatred and vengeance to all mankind. But the agony of my wound overcame me. My pulses paused, and I fainted.

"For some weeks I led a miserable life in the woods. During that time I attempted to cure my wound. The ball had entered my shoulder. I didn't know whether it had remained there or passed through. In any case, I had no means of removing it.

"My sufferings were increased also by the awful sense of the injustice and ungratefulness that brought them on. My daily vows rose for revenge. I wanted a deep and deadly revenge—the kind that would make up for the outrages and agony I had been through.

"After some weeks my wound healed, and I continued my journey. My labors were no longer eased by the bright sun or gentle breezes of spring. All joy was just a mockery which insulted my awful state. It made me feel more painfully that I was not made to enjoy pleasure.

"But my travels now drew near a close. In two

months from this time, I reached the outskirts of Geneva.

"It was evening when I arrived. I found a hiding place among the fields that surround the city. I needed time to consider how I should appeal to you. Broken down by exhaustion and hunger, I was far too unhappy to enjoy the gentle breezes of evening. I couldn't bring myself to look forward to the sun setting behind the breathtaking mountains of the Jura.

"At this time a slight sleep relieved me from my painful memories. It was disturbed by the approach of a beautiful child. With all the playfulness of childhood, he came running into the hiding place I had chosen.

"Suddenly, as I gazed on him, an idea struck me. Surely this little creature was unprejudiced. He was too young to have developed a horror of deformity. Therefore, maybe I could seize him and educate him as my companion and friend. Then I shouldn't be so alone in this peopled earth.

"Urged by this impulse, I seized on the boy as he passed and drew him towards me. As soon as he saw my form, he placed his hands before his eyes and uttered a shrill scream.

"I drew his hand from his face by force. I said, 'Child, what is the meaning of this? I don't intend to hurt you. Listen to me.'

"He struggled violently. 'Let me go,' he cried. 'Monster! Ugly wretch! You wish to eat me and tear me to pieces. You're an **ogre.** Let me go, or I'll tell my papa.'

" 'Boy,' said I, 'you'll never see your father again. You must come with me.'

" 'Hideous monster!' he cried. 'Let me go. My papa is a syndic.[1] He is M. Frankenstein. He will punish you. You dare not keep me.'

" 'Frankenstein!' I said. 'You belong then to my enemy—the one whom I have sworn eternal revenge toward. You shall be my first victim.'

---

[1] A syndic is a city official.

"The child still struggled. He loaded me with insults which carried despair to my heart. I grasped his throat to silence him. In a moment he lay dead at my feet. "I gazed on my victim, and my heart swelled with delight and hellish triumph. I clapped my hands and exclaimed, 'I too can create disaster. My enemy is not **invulnerable**. This death will carry despair to him. And a thousand other miseries shall torment and destroy him.'

"As I fixed my eyes on the child, I saw something glittering on his breast. I took it. It was a portrait of a most lovely woman. In spite of my hatred, it softened and attracted me. For a few moments I gazed on her with delight. I studied her lovely lips and her dark eyes fringed by deep lashes.

"But soon my rage returned. I remembered that I was forever kept from the delights that such beautiful creatures could give. The woman in the picture would have changed her kindly expression upon seeing me. Her face would have become twisted with disgust and fright.

"Can you wonder that such thoughts carried me away with rage? I only wonder that I was able to vent my emotions in cries of agony. Why didn't I rush among mankind and die trying to destroy them?

"While I was overcome by these feelings, I left the spot where I had committed the murder. Seeking a better hiding place, I entered a barn which had seemed empty.

"A woman was sleeping on some straw. She was young and not as beautiful as the woman whose portrait I held. But her face was agreeable. She was blooming in the loveliness of youth and health. Here, I thought, is one of those whose joy-giving smiles are given to all but me.

"And I bent over her and whispered, 'Awake, fairest. Your lover is near. I would give my life to obtain one look of affection from your eyes. My beloved, awake!'

"The sleeper stirred, and a thrill of terror ran through me. Should she indeed awake, and see me, and curse me, and accuse me as the murderer? Thus she would certainly do if her darkened eyes opened and she looked upon me.

"The thought was madness. It stirred the fiend within me. Not I, but she, shall suffer. I have committed a murder because I am forever robbed of all that she could give me. She shall **atone** for it. The crime had its source in her. Let the punishment be hers!

"Thanks to the lessons of Felix and the inhuman laws of man, I had learned now to work mischief. I bent over her and placed the portrait securely in one of the folds of her dress. She moved again, and I fled.

"For several days I haunted the spot where these scenes had taken place. Sometimes I wished to see you. Other times I wanted to leave the world and its miseries forever.

"Finally I roamed towards these mountains. I have wandered through their huge passageways filled with a burning hunger which only you can satisfy.

"We may not part until you have promised to agree to my request. I am alone and miserable, and man will have nothing to do with me. But someone as deformed and horrible as myself wouldn't deny herself to me.

"My companion must be of the same species and have the same imperfections. You must create this being."

Chapter 17

The being finished speaking and looked at me. I knew he expected a reply. But I was bewildered and **perplexed.** I couldn't think clearly enough to understand exactly what it was he wanted.

He continued, "You must create a female for me with whom I can live and share my feelings. Only you can do this. I demand it of you as a right which you must not refuse to give."

My anger had died away while he narrated his peaceful life among the cottagers. But the latter part of his tale had again inflamed my fury. I could no longer keep down the rage that burned within me.

"I do refuse it," I replied. "And no torture shall ever force an agreement from me. You may make me the most miserable of men. But you shall never make me a coward in my own eyes.

"Shall I create another like yourself so that your combined wickedness might ruin the world? Go away! I have answered you. You may torture me, but I will never consent."

"You are in the wrong," replied the fiend. "And instead of threatening, I am content to reason with you. I am cruel because I am miserable. Am I not avoided and hated by all mankind? Even you, my creator, would tear me to pieces and rejoice.

"Remember that, and tell me why I should pity man more than he pities me? You wouldn't call it murder if you could hurl me into one of those ice rifts and destroy me. And I'm the work of your own hands!

"Shall I respect man when he despises me? Let him live with me in kindness. Instead of injury, I would help him all I could. And I would shed tears of thanks at his acceptance.

"But that can't be. The human senses are **insurmountable** barriers to our union. Yet I shall not surrender like a lowly slave. I will revenge my injuries. If I can't inspire love, I will cause fear.

"I will do so especially towards you—my biggest enemy—because you are my creator. I swear unending hatred towards you. Have a care. I'll work at your destruction. And I won't quit until I ruin your heart. You shall curse the hour of your birth."

A devilish rage moved him as he said this. His face was wrinkled into shapes too horrible for human eyes to behold. But soon he calmed himself and continued.

"I intended to reason with you," he said. "This passion will do me no good. For you don't imagine that *you* are the cause of it. If only some being felt emotions of kindness towards me. I should return them a hundred and a hundredfold. For that one creature's sake I would make peace with all! But I now indulge in dreams of happiness that can't come true.

"What I ask of you is reasonable and sensible," he continued. "I demand a creature of another sex, but one as hideous as myself. The **gratification** is small. But it is all that I can have, and it shall content me.

"It is true that we shall be monsters, cut off from all the world. But for that reason we shall be more attached to one another. Our lives won't be happy. But they will be harmless and free from the misery I now feel.

"Oh! My creator, make me happy. Let me feel gratitude towards you for one kind act! Let me see that I cause the sympathy of some living thing. Don't deny my request!"

I was moved. I shuddered when I thought of the possible results of my agreement. But I felt that there was some justice in his argument.

His tale and the feelings he now expressed showed he was a creature of mature emotions. And didn't I—as his maker—owe him any happiness I could give him?

He saw my change of feeling and continued, "If you agree, neither you nor any other human being shall ever see us again. I'll go to the great wilds of South America.

"My food is not the food of man. I don't destroy the lamb and the goat to kill my appetite. Acorns and berries give me enough nourishment. My companion will be of the same nature as myself and will be content with the same food.

"We shall make our bed of dried leaves. The sun will shine on us as on man and will ripen our food. The picture I present to you is peaceful and human. Only a desire for power and cruelty could cause you to deny me.

"Pitiless as you have been towards me, I now see compassion in your eyes. Let me seize the favorable moment. Let me persuade you to promise what I so strongly desire."

"You propose," I replied, "to fly from the place where men live. You mean to dwell in those wilds where the beasts of the field will be your only companions. How can you survive in this exile? You, who long for the love and sympathy of man!

"You will return and again seek their kindness," I continued. "You will meet with their hatred, and your evil passions will be renewed. You will then have a companion to aid you in your destruction. This cannot be. Don't argue the point, for I can't agree with you."

"How changeable your feelings are!" he said. "Just a moment ago you were moved by my arguments. And why do you again harden yourself to my complaints?

"I swear this to you," he went on, "by the earth on which I live, and by you that made me. With the companion you give me, I will leave the neighborhood of man. I will live, as it may be, in the most savage of places. "My evil passions will have fled, for I shall meet with sympathy! My life will flow quietly away, and in my dying moments I shall not curse my maker."

His words had a strange effect upon me. I felt compassion for him and almost felt a wish to comfort him. But then I looked upon him and saw the filthy mass that moved and talked. My heart sickened, and my feelings were changed to those of horror and hatred.

I tried not to show my emotions. I realized that I couldn't sympathize with him. But I had no right to keep from him the small piece of happiness I could give.

"You swear to be harmless," I said. "But haven't you already shown cruelty? Shouldn't I have reason to distrust you? May not this even be a trick? And will you increase your triumph by having another to help you in your revenge?"

"How is this?" he said. "Don't treat me lightly. I demand an answer. If I have no ties and no affections, hatred and revenge must be my fate in life. The love of another will end my crimes. Then I shall become a thing whose life no one will even know of.

"My evils are the results of a forced loneliness that I hate. My virtues will necessarily take over when I live together with an equal. I shall feel the affections of a sensitive being. I shall become linked to the chain of life and events in a way which I am not now."

I paused some time to consider all of his words and arguments. I thought of the promise of goodness which he had shown at the beginning of his life. I thought, too, of the **deterioration** of all kindly feeling which followed because of the disgust and scorn he had met with. His power and threats weren't left out of my calculations. This was a creature who could live in the ice caves of the glaciers. He could hide himself among the ridges of the highest cliffs. He was a being with abilities that no human could deal with.

After a long pause of reflection, I reached a decision. The justice due both to him and my fellow creatures demanded of me that I should agree to his request.

Therefore, I turned to him and said, "I agree to your demand. But you must make a solemn oath. You shall leave Europe forever, and every other place in the neighborhood of man. You shall do so as soon as I shall give to you a female who will join you in your exile."

"I swear," he cried, "by the sun, and by the blue sky of heaven, and by the fire of love that burns my heart. If you grant my prayer, you shall never see me again as long as these things exist.

"Go home and begin your work," he went on. "I shall watch its progress with great anxiety. And don't worry. When you are ready I shall appear."

Saying this, he suddenly left me. Perhaps he feared I would change my mind. I saw him descend the mountain with greater speed than the flight of an eagle. He was quickly lost among the waves of the sea of ice.

His tale had taken up the whole day. The sun was just reaching the horizon when he departed. I knew that I ought to hurry down towards the valley. Otherwise, I should soon be **encompassed** in darkness. But my heart was heavy and my steps slow.

The task of winding among the little mountain paths and fixing my feet firmly as I went caused me to lose my way. I was too caught up in my emotions to pay attention to where I was going. Thus, night was far along when I came to the halfway resting place. I seated myself beside the fountain.

The stars shone here and there as the clouds passed

from over them. The dark pines rose before me. And every here and there a broken tree lay on the ground. The scene impressed me. And it stirred strange thoughts within me. I wept bitterly and clasped my hands in agony.

I exclaimed, "Oh! Stars and clouds and winds, you are all about to mock me. If you really pity me, crush all feeling and memory. Let me become as nothing. But if not, go away. Go away, and leave me in darkness."

These were wild and miserable thoughts. But I can't describe to you how the eternal twinkling of the stars weighed down upon me. And I listened to every blast of wind as if it were a dull, ugly siroc[1] on its way to destroy me.

Morning dawned before I arrived at the village of Chamounix. I didn't rest, but returned immediately to Geneva. Even in my own heart I couldn't give expression to my emotions. They weighed on me with a mountain's weight. And their heaviness destroyed my agony beneath them.

Thus I returned home. Entering the house, I presented myself to the family. My **haggard** and wild appearance caused extreme alarm. But I answered no question. Indeed, I hardly spoke.

I felt as if I were placed under a curse. It was as if I had no right to claim my family's sympathy. I felt I might never again enjoy companionship with them.

Yet even thus I loved them to adoration. And to save them, I decided to dedicate myself to my most hated task. The thought of such an occupation made the rest of my daily life pass before me like a dream. To me, only that thought had the reality of life.

---

[1] Siroc, or sirocco, is a hot, dusty wind which blows through parts of southern Europe.

Chapter 18 (Summary)

Frankenstein returned to Geneva. Try as he might, he could not begin working on a partner for the monster. He kept persuading himself that the task wasn't too urgent. Besides, he knew that he first needed to find out more about some scientific discoveries in England. As weeks passed, Frankenstein's health and spirits both improved. Frankenstein's father was pleased at this. He felt it was a good time to suggest that Frankenstein marry Elizabeth. Frankenstein assured his father that this would please him greatly. The older man then urged that the marriage take place immediately.

But Frankenstein remembered his last meeting with the monster. He couldn't marry Elizabeth before carrying out his promise. He had to assure the safety of his family and his future wife. To do this, he had to make a mate for the monster.

Frankenstein couldn't do such an awful thing in his family home. Since he needed information from English scientists, it seemed best to go to England. So Frankenstein arranged to tour England before his marriage. He might stay there for a few months or a year, at most. He would marry Elizabeth immediately upon his return.

Frankenstein's father considered this a good idea. Without telling Frankenstein, he and Elizabeth arranged for him to meet Clerval in Strasbourg.[1] Clerval would make the trip to England with him.

Frankenstein set out on his voyage in September. But thoughts of his coming task made him gloomy and depressed.

Then he met Clerval in Strasbourg. The two of them took a boat down the Rhine.[2] On all sides, they were

---

[1] Strasbourg is a city in northeastern France, near the French-German border.
[2] The Rhine is a European river that flows from the Swiss Alps to the North Sea. Most of it winds through Germany.

surrounded by hills, castles, towns, and the songs of laborers. Clerval was a great lover of nature. His excitement rubbed off on Frankenstein, who began to enjoy the journey.

At last they reached the sea, where they sailed for England. Late in December, they sailed up the Thames River and arrived in London.

Chapter 19 (Summary)

Frankenstein and Clerval stayed in London for several months. Clerval devoted himself to plans for a later trip to India. Frankenstein marveled at Clerval's enthusiasm. But Frankenstein wasn't nearly so happy. He contacted the English scientists and learned what he needed to know. But it was not a joyful task.

To make matters worse, Frankenstein couldn't bear to be around other people. Their happiness only made him more unhappy. The one exception was Clerval, whose eagerness and ambition reminded Frankenstein of his younger self.

Then Frankenstein received a letter from a friend in Scotland. He suggested that they come for a visit. Frankenstein and Clerval decided to go.

However, the two travelers took a long time traveling through England. It was July when they arrived at the home of Frankenstein's Scottish friend. By this time, Frankenstein was in no mood for visiting. He knew the time had come for him to keep his promise to the monster.

He began to grow fearful for his family back in Geneva. Was the monster still there, ready to murder Frankenstein's loved ones? Or had the monster followed him to England? If so, was Clerval in danger? He had no idea.

But whichever was the case, Frankenstein knew he could delay no longer. He told Clerval that he needed some time to himself—perhaps a month or so. Then he went far away to the farthest of the Orkney Islands.[1]

The island was little more than a cold and barren rock, with only five other people living on it. But this pleased Frankenstein. He wanted as few people nearby as possible while he did his dreadful work.

[1] The Orkney Islands are located off the northeast coast of Scotland.

Frankenstein longed to be done with it. He didn't doubt the monster would claim his mate the moment she was brought to life. Perhaps the monster was watching him already.

Frankenstein worked hard during the mornings. In the evenings, he tried to enjoy the sea. As every day passed, Frankenstein found the work of creating a female monster more and more hateful. But every day brought the task nearer and nearer to its finish.

Chapter 20

Vocabulary Preview

The following words appear in this chapter. Review the list and get to know the words before you read the chapter.

calamity—great misfortune; disaster
composure—self-control; coolness
grovel—squirm in shame
inhospitable—rude; impolite
loathed—felt disgust toward; hated
precarious—unsure; unsafe
quarters—housing; rooms
wily—sly; clever

I sat one evening in my laboratory. The sun had set, and the moon was just rising from the sea. I didn't have enough light for my work, and I remained still. I paused to consider whether I should leave my labor for the night or hasten its end by continuing.

As I sat, a train of memories came to me. These thoughts led me to consider the effects of what I was now doing. Three years before, I was engaged in the same work. I had then created a fiend whose unequaled evil had stricken my heart and filled it forever with the bitterest regret.

I was now about to form another being whose nature I didn't know yet. She might become ten thousand times more cruel than her mate. Perhaps she would delight in murder and misery for their own sake.

The fiend had sworn to leave the neighborhood of man and hide himself in deserts. But she hadn't. Moreover, she would most likely become a thinking and reasoning animal. Might she refuse to go along with an agreement made before her creation?

They might even hate each other. The creature who already lived **loathed** his own ugliness. Might he not be even more disgusted when it he saw it in the female form?

She also might turn with disgust from him to man's superior beauty. She might flee him, and he would be alone again. He would then be frustrated by the new torment of being deserted by his own kind.

And what if they were to leave Europe and live in the deserts of the new world? Surely one of the first results of those sympathies the demon thirsted for would be children. A race of devils would then be brought forth upon the earth. They might make the very existence of mankind **precarious** and full of terror. Had I the right— for my own benefit—to bring this curse upon future generations?

I had before been moved by the clever arguments of the being I had created. I had been struck senseless by his fiendish threats. But now, the wickedness of my promise burst upon me.

I shuddered to think that future ages might curse me as their pest. They might remember how selfishly I had hurried to buy my own peace. Perhaps that peace would have the price of the existence of the whole human race.

I trembled, and my heart failed within me. Then, on looking up, I saw by the light of the moon the demon at the window. An awful grin wrinkled his lips. He gazed on me where I sat carrying out the task which he had assigned to me.

Yes, he had followed me in my travels. He had lingered in forests, hid himself in caves, or taken refuge in wide and deserted heaths.[1] And he now came to check my progress and claim the result of my promise.

As I looked on him, his face showed the greatest

---

[1] Heaths are rough, flat lands with little growth.

possible cruelty and trickery. I felt as though I was mad to have promised to create another like him. Trembling with passion, I tore to pieces the thing on which I worked.

The wretch watched me destroy the creature whom he depended on for future happiness. With a howl of devilish despair and revenge, he departed.

I left the room and locked the door. I made a solemn vow in my own heart never to continue my work. Then, with trembling steps, I went to my own room. I was alone. No one was near me to share the gloom. No one could relieve me from the sickening burden of the most terrible memories.

Several hours passed. I remained near my window gazing on the sea. It was almost motionless, for the winds were hushed. All nature slept under the eye of the quiet moon. A few fishing boats alone dotted the water. And now and then the gentle breeze lifted the sound of voices as the fishermen called to one another.

I felt the silence, although I was hardly conscious of its great depth. Then my ear was suddenly arrested by the paddling of oars near the shore. A person landed close to my house.

A few minutes later, I heard the creaking of my door, as if someone tried to open it softly. I trembled from head to foot. I felt a suspicion of who it was. I wished to rouse one of the peasants who lived in a cottage near mine.

But I was overcome by a sensation of helplessness. It is the feeling one has in awful dreams—when one tries in vain to flee from danger but is rooted to the spot.

Soon I heard the sound of footsteps along the passage. The door opened, and the wretch whom I dreaded appeared.

Shutting the door, he approached me and said in a smothered voice, "You have destroyed the work which you began. What do you mean by this? Do you dare to break your promise?

"I have endured toil and misery," he went on. "I left Switzerland with you. I crept along the shores of the

Rhine, among its willow islands and over the tops of its hills. I have lived many months in the heaths of England and among the deserts of Scotland. I have endured terrible exhaustion and cold and hunger. Do you dare destroy my hopes?"

"Go away!" said I. "I do break my promise. Never will I create another like yourself, equal in ugliness and wickedness."

"Slave," he said, "I reasoned with you before. But you have proved yourself unworthy of my trust. Remember that I have power. You believe yourself miserable, but I can make you so wretched that the light of day will be hateful to you. You are my creator, but I am your master. Obey!"

"The hour of my indecision is past," said I. "And the period of your power is arrived. Your threats can't move me to do an act of wickedness. But they make me even more determined not to create for you a companion in evil.

"Shall I, in cool blood, do as you ask?" I continued. "Shall I set loose upon the earth a demon whose delight is in death and destruction? Begone! I am firm, and your words will only stir up my rage."

The monster saw the determination in my face. He gnashed his teeth in helpless anger.

"Shall each man find a wife for his bosom, and each beast have his mate, and I be alone?" he cried. "I had feelings of affection, and they were returned with disgust and scorn.

"Man!" he went on. "You may hate, but beware! Your hours will pass in dread and misery. And soon the bolt will fall which must tear from you your happiness forever.

"Are you to be happy while I **grovel** in my intense misery?" he said. "You can curse my other passions, but revenge remains—revenge, from now on dearer than light or food!

"I may die," the fiend continued. "But first, you—my

tyrant and tormentor—shall curse the sun that gazes on your misery. Beware, for I am fearless and therefore powerful. I will watch you like a **wily** snake, that I may sting with its poison. You shall be sorry for the injuries you caused."

"Devil, stop," I said. "Don't poison the air with these sounds of cruelty. I have declared my decision to you. And I am no coward to bend beneath words. Leave me. I won't change my mind."

"It is well," he said. "I go. But remember, I shall be with you on your wedding night."

I started forward and exclaimed, "Villain! Before you sign my death warrant, be sure that you are safe yourself."

I would have grabbed him. But he escaped me and left the house in a hurry. In a few moments I saw him in his boat. It shot across the waters as swiftly as an arrow. Soon it was lost among the waves.

All was silent again, but his words rang in my ears. I burned with rage. I wanted to go after the murderer of my peace and hurl him into the ocean. I walked up and down my room with quick steps. I was very upset. A thousand images tormented and stung me in my imagination.

Why hadn't I followed him and wrestled with him in mortal struggle? But I had allowed him to go. And he had directed his boat towards the mainland.

I shuddered to think who might be the next victim of his unsatisfied revenge. And then I thought again of his words—*"I will be with you on your wedding night."* That, then, was the moment that would decide my fate. In that hour I should die. His cruelty would at once be satisfied and ended.

I felt no fear at the prospect. Yet I thought of my beloved Elizabeth—of her tears and endless sorrow—when she should find her lover so cruelly snatched from her. The first tears I had shed for many months streamed from my eyes. I decided not to fall before my enemy without a bitter struggle.

The night passed away, and the sun rose from the ocean. My feelings became calmer. That is, if it may be called calmness when rage sinks into despair. I left the house, the horrid scene of the last night's quarrel. I walked on the beach of the sea. I almost regarded water as a complete barrier between me and my fellow creatures.

Indeed, a wish that this might prove true stole across me. I desired that I might spend my life on that lonely rock. I would do so wearily, it is true. But at least I wouldn't be interrupted by any sudden shock of misery. If I returned to civilization, I would be sacrificed. Or I would live only to see those whom I most loved die. Either would be done at the hands of a demon whom I had created myself.

I walked about the island like a restless spirit. I was separated from all I loved and miserable in the separation. It became noon, and the sun rose higher. I lay down on the grass and was overpowered by a deep sleep.

I had been awake the whole of the night before. My nerves were wound up, and my eyes inflamed by watching and misery. The sleep into which I now sank refreshed me. And when I awoke, I again felt as if I belonged to a race of human beings like myself.

With greater **composure,** I began to think back upon what had happened. Yet still the words of the fiend rang in my ears like a funeral bell. They appeared like a dream, yet clear and harsh as a reality.

The sun had gone way down, and I still sat on the shore. I had become very hungry and was eating an oat cake. Then I saw a fishing boat land close to me, and one of the men brought me a packet.

It contained letters from Geneva and one from Clerval begging me to join him. He said that he was spending his time uselessly where he was. Letters from friends he had made in London asked him to return. They wanted Clerval to complete the plans he had begun concerning his trip to India.

Clerval wrote that he couldn't put off his departure any longer. But his journey to London might soon be followed by his longer voyage to India. Therefore, he wanted me to spend as much time with him as I could. So he asked me to leave my lonely island and to meet him at Perth.[2] Then we might go on southwards together.

This letter somewhat recalled me to life. I decided to leave my island at the end of two days.

Yet, before I left, there was a task to perform. I shuddered to think of it. I must pack up my chemical instruments. And to do that I must enter the room which had been the scene of my hateful work. I must handle those instruments, though the sight of them sickened me.

The next morning, at daybreak, I got up enough courage and unlocked the door of my laboratory. The remains of the half-finished creature whom I had destroyed lay scattered on the floor. I almost felt as if I had torn to pieces the living flesh of a human being.

I paused to collect myself and then entered the room. With trembling hands I carried the chemical tools out of the room. But I thought that I shouldn't leave the remains of my work there. I had no wish to stir up the horror and suspicion of the peasants.

Therefore, I put the remains into a basket, along with a large number of stones. I put the basket away, determined to throw it into the sea that very night. In the meantime I sat upon the beach. I busied myself with cleaning and arranging my chemical instruments.

Nothing could be more complete than the change in my feelings since the night the demon appeared. Before, I had regarded my promise with gloomy despair. I thought it a thing that must be done, no matter what the result.

But now I felt as if a film had been taken from before my eyes. For the first time I saw clearly. The idea of starting work again on a female fiend never once

---

[2] Perth is a city in east-central Scotland.

occurred to me. The threat I had heard weighed on my thoughts. But I didn't think that any act of mine could change it.

I had decided in my own mind that I couldn't create another like the fiend I had first made. That would be the most wicked and unspeakable selfish act. I got rid of every thought that could possibly change my feelings.

Between two and three in the morning the moon rose. I then put my basket aboard a small boat and sailed out about four miles from the shore. The scene was perfectly lonely. A few boats were returning towards land, but I sailed away from them. I felt as if I was about to commit a dreadful crime. I nervously avoided any meeting with my fellow creatures.

At one time the moon was suddenly covered by a thick cloud. I took advantage of the darkness and threw my basket into the sea. I listened to the gurgling sound as it sank. Then I sailed away from the spot.

The sky became clouded. But the air was pure, although chilled by the northeast breeze that was rising then. The breeze refreshed me and filled me with pleasant feelings. I soon decided to stay on the water a while longer. I fixed my rudder[3] in a direct position and stretched myself at the bottom of the boat.

Clouds hid the moon and everything was dark. I heard only the sound of the boat as its keel[4] cut through the waves. The murmur calmed me. In a short time I slept soundly.

I don't know how long I remained like this. But when I awoke I found that the sun had already risen quite high. The wind was strong. And the waves continually threatened the safety of my little boat. I found that the wind was northeast and must have driven me far from the coast from which I had taken off.

I tried to change my course. But I quickly found that

---

[3] A rudder controls the direction of a boat or ship.
[4] The keel is the ridge which extends along the bottom of a boat from front to back.

if I tried that again, the boat would be instantly filled with water. In this situation, my only hope was to drive before the wind.

I confess that I felt some terror. I had no compass with me and didn't know the geography of this part of the world very well. So the location of the sun was of little help to me.

I might be driven into the wide Atlantic and starve. Or I might be swallowed up in the great waves that roared and crashed around me. I had already been out many hours and felt the torment of a burning thirst. This was the beginning of my other sufferings.

I looked up at the heavens. They were covered by clouds that flew before the wind, only to be replaced by others. I looked upon the sea. It was to be my grave.

"Fiend," I exclaimed, "your task is already fulfilled!"

I thought of Elizabeth, of my father, and of Clerval— all left behind. On them the monster might satisfy his bloodthirsty and merciless rage. The very idea plunged me into a hopeless and frightful state. The scene is about to close before me forever. Yet even now I shudder to remember it.

Some hours passed in this way. But gradually the sun descended towards the horizon. The wind died away into a gentle breeze. Then the sea became free from violent waves. But these gave place to a heavy swell.[5] I felt sick and hardly able to hold the rudder. At last I suddenly saw a line of high land towards the south.

I was exhausted from the dreadful suspense I had endured for several hours. So this sudden sign of life rushed like a flood of warm joy to my heart. Tears gushed from my eyes.

How changeable our feelings are! How strange is that clinging love we have of life, even in the greatest misery! I put together another sail with a part of my clothing. Then I eagerly steered my course towards the land.

[5] *Swell* refers to big, long waves that continue one after the other.

It had a wild and rocky appearance. But as I approached nearer, I easily saw the traces of human life. I saw boats near the shore and found myself brought back to the neighborhood of civilized man. I carefully looked at the paths on the land. I cheered at the sight of a steeple which appeared from behind a hill. As I was extremely weak, I decided to sail directly towards the town. I would most easily find food there. Fortunately I had money with me.

As I turned past the hill I spotted a small, neat town and a good harbor. I entered it, my heart bounding with joy at my unexpected escape from the cruel sea.

As I was busy fixing the boat and arranging the sails, several people crowded towards the spot. They seemed much surprised at my appearance. But instead of offering me any help, they whispered together. Their gestures might have caused alarm in me at any other time. As it was, I merely noticed that they spoke English. Therefore, I addressed them in that language.

"My good friends," said I, "will you be so kind as to tell me the name of this town and where I am?"

"You will know that soon enough," replied a man with a rough voice. "Maybe you've come to a place you won't much like. But you won't have any choice as to your **quarters,** I promise you."

I was very surprised on receiving such a rude answer from a stranger. I was also disturbed on seeing the frowning and angry faces of his companions.

"Why do you answer me so roughly?" I replied. "Surely it's not the custom of Englishmen to be so **inhospitable** to strangers."

"I don't know what the custom of the English may be," said the man. "But it is the custom of the Irish to hate villains."

While this strange conversation continued, the crowd quickly grew. Their faces expressed a mixture of curiosity and anger. I felt annoyed and somewhat alarmed.

I asked the way to the inn, but no one replied. I then

moved forward. A murmuring sound arose from the crowd as they followed and surrounded me. At last, an ill-looking man approached and tapped me on the shoulder. "Come, sir," he said. "You must follow me to Mr. Kirwin's to explain yourself."

"Who is Mr. Kirwin?" I asked. "And why am I to explain myself? Isn't this a free country?"

"Aye, sir, free enough for honest folks," replied the man. "Mr. Kirwin is a magistrate. You are to explain the death of a gentleman who was found murdered here last night."

This answer startled me, but I quickly recovered myself. I was innocent. That could easily be proved. So I followed my guide in silence and was led to one of the best houses in the town.

I was ready to sink from exhaustion and hunger. But as I was surrounded by the crowd, I thought it wise to rouse all my strength. I wanted to show no sign of weakness that might be thought of as nervousness or guilt.

Little did I expect the **calamity** that was to overwhelm me in a few moments. The horror and despair of it would end all fear of shame or death.

I must pause here. It requires all my courage to recall the memory of these frightful events. But I will try to tell of them, in proper detail, as well as I can remember them.

Chapter 21

Vocabulary Preview

The following words appear in this chapter. Review the list and get to know the words before you read the chapter.

coincidences—accidental events that seem to be related; chance happenings
persecuted—tormented; harassed
ravings—wild or hysterical speech; meaningless words
relapse—setback; turn for the worse
squalid—extremely dirty; filthy
testify—give information sworn to be true; state under oath

I was soon brought before the magistrate, Mr. Kirwin. He was a kindly old man with calm and mild manners. However, he looked upon me somewhat severely. Then he turned towards my guides and asked who appeared as witnesses on this occasion.

About a half a dozen men came forward. One was selected by the magistrate to **testify.** This man said he had been out fishing the night before with his son and brother-in-law, Daniel Nugent. At about ten o'clock, they observed a strong northerly wind rising. So they headed for shore.

It was a very dark night, as the moon hadn't risen yet. They didn't land at the harbor, but at a creek about two miles below, as they often did. He walked on first, carrying a part of the fishing tackle. His companions followed him at some distance.

As he was going along the sands, he struck his foot against something and fell flat on the ground. His companions came up to help him. By the light of their lantern, they found that he had fallen on the body of a man who seemed to be dead.

Their first guess was that it was the corpse of someone who had been drowned and then thrown on shore by the waves. But upon inspection they found that the clothes weren't wet. The body wasn't even cold then.

They instantly carried it to the cottage of an old woman near the spot. There they tried in vain to restore it to life. It appeared to be a handsome young man, about twenty-five years of age. He had apparently been strangled. There was no sign of any violence except the black mark of fingers on his neck.

The first part of this testimony didn't interest me in the least. But then the mark of the fingers was mentioned. I remembered my brother's murder and became very upset. My limbs trembled, and a mist came over my eyes. I had to lean on a chair for support.

The magistrate looked at me with a sharp eye. He, of course, became suspicious at my manner.

The son confirmed his father's story. But when Daniel Nugent was called he swore positively that he saw a boat just before his companion fell. It had one man in it and was a short distance from the shore. As far as he could tell by the light of a few stars, it was the same boat in which I had just landed.

A woman testified that she lived near the beach. She had been standing at the door of her cottage about an hour before she heard about the body. She was waiting for the fishermen to return. At that time she saw a boat with only one man in it. The boat pushed off from the shore where the corpse was afterwards found.

Another woman confirmed that the fishermen had brought the body into her house. The body wasn't cold. They put it into a bed and rubbed it. Daniel went to the town for an apothecary.[1] But it was obvious that life was quite gone.

Several other men were questioned concerning my landing. They agreed that the strong north wind had arisen during the night. So it was very probable that I had whipped about for many hours. Then I might have been forced to return nearly to the same spot from which I had left.

Besides, they observed that it appeared that I had brought the body from another place. I didn't seem to know the shore. So it was likely that I might have come into the harbor on my way to the town of ——.[2] I wouldn't have known how far the town was from the place where I had left the corpse.

Mr. Kirwin listened to this evidence. Then he asked that I be taken into the room where the body lay waiting for burial. He wanted to see what effect the sight of it would have on me.

The magistrate had seen how disturbed I had become when the method of murder had been described. That is probably where his idea came from. Therefore, I was led to the inn by the magistrate and several other persons.

I couldn't help being struck by the strange **coincidences** that had taken place during this eventful night. But I knew that I had talked with several people on the island I had been living on. This had been about the time that the body had been found. So I was perfectly calm about how things would turn out.

I entered the room where the corpse lay and was led up to the coffin. How can I describe my reaction on looking at it? I still shrink with horror. Even now I can't remember that terrible moment without shuddering and agony.

The questioning, the presence of the magistrate and witnesses—all passed from my memory like a dream. For

---

[1] An apothecary is a pharmacist.
[2] Many early authors followed the custom of not writing a full name of a place or person. Sometimes writers placed initials before the dashes.

I saw the lifeless form of Henry Clerval stretched before me. I gasped for breath and threw myself on the body.

I exclaimed, "Have my murderous plans caused your death also, my dearest Henry? I have already destroyed two. And other victims await their fate. But you, Clerval, my friend who meant for me only good—"

The human frame could no longer support the agonies I endured. I was carried out of the room, shaking terribly.

A fever came after this. I lay for two months on the point of death. My **ravings** were frightful, as I afterwards heard. I called myself the murderer of William, of Justine, and of Clerval.

Sometimes I begged those who attended me to help me destroy the fiend who tormented me. At other times I felt the fingers of the monster already grasping my neck. I screamed aloud with agony and terror.

Fortunately, I spoke my native language. So only Mr. Kirwin understood me. But my gestures and bitter cries were enough to frighten the other witnesses.

Why didn't I die? I was more miserable than man ever was before. Why didn't I sink into forgetfulness and rest?

Death snatches away many blooming children, the only hopes of their loving parents. And how many brides and youthful lovers have fallen? One minute they are in the bloom of health and hope. The next they're food for worms and the decay of the tomb!

What was I made of that I could thus resist so many shocks? These shocks constantly renewed the torture like the turning of a wheel.

But I was doomed to live. And in two months, I found myself as if waking up from a dream. I was in a prison, stretched on an uncomfortable bed. I was surrounded by jailers, turnkeys,³ bolts, and all the miserable devices of a dungeon.

---

³ Turnkeys are guards in charge of a prison's keys.

I remember it was morning when I thus awoke. I had forgotten exactly what had happened. I only felt as if some great misfortune had suddenly overwhelmed me. But then I looked around and saw the barred windows and the **squalid** room where I lay. Then everything flashed across my memory, and I groaned bitterly.

The sound disturbed an old woman who was sleeping in a chair beside me. She was a hired nurse, the wife of one of the turnkeys. In her face were all those bad qualities which often belong to that class.

The lines of her face where hard and rude. They were like that of persons used to looking on misery with no sympathy. Her tone expressed her entire uncaring attitude.

She addressed me in English. The voice struck me as one that I had heard during my sufferings.

"Are you better now, sir?" said she.

I replied in the same language, with a weak voice, "I believe I am. But is it all true? Did I not dream? If it wasn't a dream, I'm sorry that I'm still alive to feel this misery and horror."

"You must mean the gentleman you murdered," replied the old woman. "If so, I believe it were better for you if you were dead. For I fancy it will go hard with you!

"However," she continued, "that's none of my business. I am sent to nurse you and get you well. I do my duty with a safe conscience. It were well if everybody did the same."

I turned with dislike from the woman. How could she speak with so little feeling to a person just saved, on the very edge of death? But I felt weak and unable to think about all that had passed.

My whole life appeared to me as a dream. I sometimes doubted if indeed it were all true. For it never hit my mind with the force of reality.

As the images that floated before me became clearer, I grew feverish. A darkness pressed around me. No one was nearby to soothe me with the gentle voice of love. No dear hand supported me.

The doctor came and prescribed medicines. The old woman prepared them for me. But total carelessness was visible in the doctor. And cruelty was strongly marked in the face of the woman. Who could be interested in the fate of a murderer but the hangman who would gain his fee?

These were my first thoughts. But I soon learned that Mr. Kirwin had shown me extreme kindness. He had caused the best room in the prison to be prepared for me. Though dark and cheerless, it was indeed the best. And it was he who had provided a doctor and a nurse.

It's true he seldom came to see me. He strongly desired to relieve the sufferings of every human creature. But he didn't wish to be present at the agonies and miserable ravings of a murderer.

Therefore, he sometimes came to see that I wasn't neglected. But his visits were short and rare.

One day, while I was gradually recovering, I was seated in a chair. My eyes were half open and my cheeks pale like those in death. I was overcome by gloom and misery. I thought that I ought to seek death. Better that than to wish to remain in a world which to me was full of misery.

At one time I wondered whether I shouldn't declare myself guilty. Then I should suffer the penalty of the law. And at least I would be less innocent than poor Justine had been.

These were my thoughts when the door of my cell was opened and Mr. Kirwin entered. His face expressed sympathy and compassion. He drew a chair close to mine and addressed me in French.

"I fear that this place is very shocking to you," he said. "Can I do anything to make you more comfortable?"

"I thank you," I replied. "But all that you speak of means nothing to me. On the whole earth there is no comfort which I am capable of receiving."

"I can only offer you the sympathy of a stranger," Mr. Kirwin said. "That can be but of little relief to one burdened as you are by so strange a misfortune. But I hope you will soon leave this depressing place. For no doubt evidence can easily be brought to free you from the criminal charge."

"That is my least concern," I said. "By a course of strange events, I have become the most miserable of human beings. I am and have been **persecuted** and tortured. Can death be any evil to me?"

"Strange coincidences have occurred lately," he said. "Indeed, nothing could be more unfortunate and painful. By some surprising accident, you were thrown on this shore, which is famous for its hospitality.

"Then you were seized immediately and charged with murder. The first sight that was shown to you was the body of your friend. He was murdered in an unexplainable manner and placed across your path by some fiend, as it were."

As Mr. Kirwin began his retelling of my sufferings, I became upset. But I also felt quite some surprise at the knowledge he seemed to have concerning me.

I suppose some astonishment was visible on my face. For Mr. Kirwin hurried to say, "Immediately after you took ill, all the papers that were found on you were brought to me. I examined them. I hoped to discover how I could notify your family of your misfortune and illness.

"I found several letters. Among others was one which I discovered to be from your father. I instantly wrote to Geneva. Nearly two months have gone since I sent my letter.

"But you are ill," he continued. "Even now you tremble. You are unfit for excitement of any kind."

"This suspense is a thousand times worse than the most horrible event," I said. "Tell me what new scene of death has been acted. Whose murder am I now to mourn for?"

"Your family is perfectly well," said Mr. Kirwin gently. "And someone, a friend, has come to visit you."

I don't know how I got the idea. But it instantly darted into my mind that the murderer had come to mock at my misery. He wished to taunt me with Clerval's death. This would be a new way to get me to go along with his hellish desires.

I put my hand before my eyes and cried out in agony.

"Oh! Take him away!" I said. "I can't see him. For God's sake, don't let him enter!"

Mr. Kirwin looked at me with a troubled expression. He couldn't help seeing my exclamation as an admission of my guilt. So he said in rather a severe tone, "Young man, I should have thought that your father's presence would have been welcome. But instead it has inspired violent disgust."

"My father!" I cried. Every feature and every muscle was relaxed from pain to pleasure. "Is my father indeed come? How kind, how very kind! But where is he? Why doesn't he hurry to me?"

My change of manner surprised and pleased the magistrate. Perhaps he thought that my former outburst was a short return of my madness. And now he instantly took on his former kind look. He rose and left the room with my nurse. In a moment my father entered.

At this moment, nothing could have given me greater pleasure than my father's arrival. I stretched out my hand to him and cried, "Are you safe, then—and Elizabeth—and Ernest?"

My father calmed me with assurances of their well-being. He tried to raise my spirits by dwelling on the subject of my brother and cousin. But he soon felt that a prison can't be the place for cheerfulness. He looked mournfully at the barred windows and gloomy appearance of the room.

"What a place this is that you're in, my son!" said he. "You traveled to seek happiness, but a death seems to follow you. And poor Clerval—"

The name of my unfortunate and murdered friend greatly disturbed me. It was too much to endure in my weak state. I shed tears.

"Alas! Yes, my father," I replied. "Some destiny of the most horrible kind hangs over me. And I was meant to fulfill my fate. Otherwise, I should have died on Henry's coffin."

We weren't allowed to talk for a very long time. My health was uncertain. So every precaution was necessary to ensure that I stayed calm.

Mr. Kirwin came in and insisted that too much strain would exhaust my strength. But the appearance of my father was like that of my good angel to me. I gradually recovered my health.

As my sickness left me, I became filled with a gloomy and black depression. Nothing could rid me of it. Clerval's image was forever before me, ghastly and murdered. More than once my thoughts caused me to become greatly disturbed. My friends feared I would suffer a dangerous **relapse.**

Alas! Why did they preserve such a miserable and hated life? It was surely that I might fulfill my fate, which is now drawing close. Soon, oh, very soon, death will end my sufferings. It will relieve me from the mighty pain that pushes me to the ground. Death will bring me justice, and I shall also sink to rest.

Back then, death itself seemed far away, though I wished for it many times. I often sat for hours motionless and speechless. I wished for some awful thing to happen that might bury me and that fiend in its ruins.

The time for my trial arrived. I had already been in prison for three months. I was still weak and in constant danger of a relapse. Even so, I was forced to travel nearly a hundred miles to the country town where the court was held.

Mr. Kirwin gave the greatest care to collecting witnesses and arranging my defense. As it turned out, I was spared the disgrace of appearing publicly as a criminal. For the case was not brought before the court that decides on life and death after all.

The grand jury[4] dismissed the case, as it was proved that I was on the Orkney Islands at the time my friend's body was found. And two weeks after my removal, I was freed from prison.

My father was delighted on finding me freed from the trouble of a criminal charge. He was pleased that I was again allowed to breathe the fresh air and permitted to return home. I didn't share in these feelings. For to me, the walls of a dungeon or a palace were both hateful. The cup of life was poisoned forever.

True, the sun shone upon me as upon the happy and gay of heart. But I saw nothing around me but a deep, frightful darkness. No light entered except for the glimmer of two eyes that glared upon me. Sometimes they were the expressive eyes of Henry, wasting in death. His dark eyes were nearly covered by the lids and the long black lashes that fringed them. Other times I saw the watery, clouded eyes of the monster. They looked just as I first saw them in my room at Ingolstadt.

My father tried to awaken feelings of affection in me. He talked of Geneva, which I should soon visit. And he spoke of Elizabeth and Ernest. But these words only drew deep groans from me.

Indeed, sometimes I felt a wish for happiness. I thought with sad delight of my beloved cousin. I also became very homesick. I longed to see once more the blue lake and the rapid Rhone. They had been very dear to me in my early childhood.

But generally, I felt only a dullness of mind. To me, a prison was as welcome a place to stay as the most majestic scene in nature. These feelings were rarely interrupted except by rages of pain and despair.

At these moments I often tried to put an end to my life. It required nonstop care and watchfulness to keep

---

[4] A grand jury studies the charges against a person in order to decide whether a trial should be held.

me from committing some dreadful act of violence.

Yet one duty was still required of me. Remembering it finally triumphed over my selfish despair. It was necessary that I should return at once to Geneva. There I would watch over the lives of those I so fondly loved. And there I would lie in wait for the murderer.

Perhaps a chance would lead me to the fiend's hiding place. Or perhaps he would dare again to curse me with his presence. With perfect aim, I might then put an end to a monstrous image and an even more monstrous soul.

My father still wanted to put off our departure. He was fearful that I couldn't endure an exhausting journey. For I was a shattered wreck—just a shadow of a human being. My strength was gone. I was a mere skeleton, and fever preyed upon my wasted body night and day.

Still, I urged our leaving Ireland quite strongly and impatiently. Finally, my father thought it best to give in. We took our passage on a boat bound for Havre-de-Grâce⁵ and sailed with a fair wind from the Irish shores.

It was midnight. I lay on the deck looking at the stars and listening to the dashing of the waves. I welcomed the darkness that shut Ireland from my sight. My pulse beat with a feverish joy when I realized that I should soon see Geneva.

The past appeared to me as a frightful dream. Yet I knew all those horrible events had really happened. True, I was in a boat being carried away from the hated shore of Ireland. Only the sea now surrounded me. But still, Clerval—my friend and dearest companion—had fallen a victim to me and the monster I had created.

I looked back through my memory over my whole life. I remembered my quiet happiness while living with my family in Geneva. I remembered, too, my mother's death and my departure for Ingolstadt.

Shuddering, I remembered the mad enthusiasm that hurried me on the creation of my hideous enemy. I called

---

⁵ Havre-de-Grâce is a seaport in northwestern France. It is now known simply as Le Havre.

to mind the night in which he first lived. But I was unable to follow that train of thought. A thousand feelings pressed upon me, and I wept bitterly.

I had recovered from the fever. Since then I had been in the custom of taking a small quantity of laudanum[6] every night. Only by using this drug was I able to gain the rest I needed to go on living. The memories of my various misfortunes troubled me. So I now swallowed double my usual quantity and soon slept deeply.

But sleep didn't give me rest from thought and misery. My dreams presented a thousand objects that scared me. Towards morning I was possessed by a kind of nightmare. I felt the fiend's grasp in my neck and couldn't free myself from it. Groans and cries rang in my ears.

My father was watching over me. He noticed my restlessness and awoke me. I opened my eyes and saw the dashing waves around me and the cloudy sky above. The fiend was not here.

I felt a sense of security. It was as if peace had been made between the present hour and the certain future of disaster. I became filled with a calm forgetfulness—the kind that makes the human mind become helpless, in a strange way.

[6] Laudanum is a sleep-inducing drug made from opium.

Chapter 22

Vocabulary Preview

The following words appear in this chapter. Review the list and get to know the words before you read the chapter.

devoid—empty; lacking
incurable—unable to be healed; hopeless
sinister—dangerous; evil
woe—deep sadness; misery

The voyage came to an end. We landed and went on to Paris. I soon found that I had worn out my strength. So I had to rest before I could continue my journey.

My father's care and attentions were endless. But he didn't know the real reason for my sufferings. So he tried all the wrong methods to heal the **incurable** ill. He wanted me to seek amusement in society, but I hated the face of man.

Oh, not hated! They were my brothers and my fellow beings. And I was drawn toward even the most offensive among them. It was as if they were like angels, with heavenly qualities. But I felt that I had no right to share in their talk.

I had let an enemy loose among them. And it was his joy to shed their blood and to rejoice in their groans. What if they knew my unholy acts and the crimes which began with me? Surely each and every one of them would despise me and wish me dead.

At last, my father gave in to my wish to avoid society. He tried to get rid of my despair with various arguments.

Sometimes he thought that I deeply felt the shame of having to answer a murder charge. And he tried to prove to me the uselessness of pride.

"Alas! My father," said I, "how little you know me. Human beings—and their feelings and passions—would indeed be worthless if such a wretch as I felt pride.

"Justine, poor, unhappy Justine," I went on. "She was as innocent as I, and she suffered the same charge. She died for it. And I am the cause of this—I murdered her. William, Justine, and Henry—they all died by my hands."

My father had often heard me say the same thing during my imprisonment. When I thus accused myself, he sometimes seemed to want an explanation. And at others he appeared to consider it as the result of madness.

I suppose he thought that during my illness some idea of this kind had entered my imagination. And he guessed I still believed it now that I had gotten well.

I avoided explanation and kept silent about the wretch I had created. I was sure that I should be thought mad. This in itself would forever have chained my tongue.

But besides, I couldn't bring myself to reveal a secret which would fill my listener with dread. It would burden him with fear and unnatural horror. Therefore, I held back my impatient thirst for sympathy. I was silent when I would have given anything to have confided the fatal secret.

Yet still, words like those I have just spoken of would burst uncontrollably from me. I couldn't explain them. But their truth partly relieved the burden of my mysterious **woe.**

Upon one occasion, my father displayed an expression of endless wonder.

"My dearest Victor," he said, "what madness is this? My dear son, I beg you never to make such a claim again."

"I'm not mad," I cried forcefully. "The sun and the heavens have viewed my activities. They can bear witness to my truth. I am the murderer of those most innocent victims. They died by my devices.

"I would have shed my own blood a thousand times to have saved their lives," I went on. "But I couldn't, my father. Indeed, I couldn't even sacrifice the whole human race."

The end of this speech convinced my father that my ideas were mad. So he instantly changed the subject of our conversation and tried to move my thoughts in another direction. He wished to erase as much as possible the memory of the scenes that had taken place in Ireland. He never mentioned them or allowed me to speak of my misfortunes.

As time passed away I became more calm. Misery still dwelled in my heart. But I no longer talked in the same wild manner of my own crimes. It was enough for me that I was aware of them.

The urgent voice of despair sometimes desired to declare itself to the whole world. But I held it back using the greatest self-violence. And my manners were calmer and more in control than they had ever been since my journey to the sea of ice.

A few days before we left Paris on our way to Switzerland, I received the following letter from Elizabeth:

My dear Friend,

It gave me the greatest pleasure to receive a letter from my uncle dated at Paris. You are no longer so far away. Now I may hope to see you in less than two weeks.

My poor cousin, how much you must have suffered! I expect to see you looking even more ill than when you left Geneva. This winter has been spent most miserably. I have been tortured by anxious suspense.

Yet I hope to see peace in your face. And I hope to find that your heart isn't totally **devoid** of comfort and calmness.

However, I fear that you still have the same feelings that made you so miserable a year ago. Perhaps they've even grown greater with time. I wouldn't disturb you now, when so many misfortunes weigh upon you. But I had a conversation with my uncle before he left. And I need to explain something before we meet.

Explain! You may possibly say, "What can Elizabeth have to explain?" If you really say this, my questions are answered, and all my doubts satisfied.

But you are far away from me. It's possible that you may dread and yet be pleased with this explanation. Since this is probably the case, I dare not put off writing to you any longer. During your absence, I have often wished to express this to you. But I've never had the courage to begin.

Victor, you well know that our marriage had been the favorite plan of your parents ever since our childhood. We were told this when young. And we were taught to look forward to it as an event that would certainly take place.

We were affectionate playmates during childhood. And I believe we were dear and valued friends to one another as we grew older. But a brother and sister often feel a lively affection towards each other without wanting a closer union. Could this also be our case?

Tell me, dearest Victor. I beg you to answer me with the simple truth. Happiness for both of us depends on it. Do you not love another?

You have traveled. You have spent several years of your life at Ingolstadt. And I confess something to you, my friend. I saw you last autumn so unhappy, rushing to be alone, to be away from the society of every creature. And I couldn't help thinking that you might regret our relationship.

I wondered if you believed yourself bound in honor to fulfill your parents' wishes. And perhaps these wishes went against your own desires.

But this is false reasoning. I confess to you, my friend, that I love you. In my airy dreams of the future, you have been my constant friend and companion.

But I desire your happiness as well as my own. So I must tell you that our marriage would make me forever miserable unless it occurred out of your own free choice. Even now I weep to think how held down you are by the worst misfortunes. I can't bear to think you might smother all hopes of love and happiness in the name of honor.

I have the deepest affection for you. But even so, I realize I may increase your miseries ten times by standing in the way of your wishes. Ah! Victor, be assured that your cousin and playmate has a very sincere love for you. And I am made miserable by the thought that you may not feel the same.

Be happy, my friend, and obey me in this one request. Remain satisfied that nothing on earth will have the power to disturb my peace.

Don't let this letter upset you. Don't answer it tomorrow, or the next day, or even until you come, if it will give you pain. My uncle will send me news of your health. And I hope to see at least one smile on your lips when we meet. If this smile is caused by this letter or any other effort of mine, I shall need no other happiness.

Elizabeth Lavenza
Geneva, May 18th, 17—

This letter awoke in my memory what I had forgotten before. It was the threat of the fiend: *"I will be with you on your wedding night!"*

That was the sentence pronounced upon me. And on that night the demon would attempt every trick to destroy me. He'd tear me from the glimpse of happiness which promised partly to relieve my sufferings. On that night he would be determined to complete his crimes by my death.

Well, let him try. A deadly struggle would then certainly take place. If he were victorious, his power over me should be at an end. If he were defeated, I should be a free man.

Alas! What freedom? Such as the peasant enjoys when his family has been killed, his cottage burnt, and his lands laid waste. Though he is turned adrift, homeless, penniless, and alone, he is free.

Such would be my liberty. However, I possessed a treasure in my Elizabeth. Alas, she would be balanced by those horrors of regret and guilt which would follow me until death.

Sweet and beloved Elizabeth! I read and reread her letter. And some softened feelings stole into my heart. They dared to whisper dreams of a paradise of love and joy. But the apple was already eaten, and the angel's arm bared to drive me away from all hope.[1] Yet I would die to make her happy.

If the monster carried out his threat, death was certain. Yet again, I considered whether my marriage would hurry my fate. My destruction might indeed arrive a few months sooner. But what if my torturer should suspect that—scared of his threats—I should delay the wedding? He would surely find other and perhaps more dreadful means of revenge.

He had vowed *to be with me on my wedding night.* Yet he didn't feel that his threat should keep him from other evil. He wanted to show me that his thirst for blood wasn't yet satisfied. So he had murdered Clerval immediately after he made his threats.

I could see that my immediate union with my cousin would add to my father's and her happiness. So my enemy's plans against my life shouldn't delay it a single hour.

In this state of mind I wrote to Elizabeth. My letter was calm and affectionate.

"My beloved girl," I said, "I fear little happiness remains for us on earth. Yet all that I may one day enjoy is centered on you. Chase away your foolish fears. To you

---

[1] In *Paradise Lost,* Adam and Eve ate an apple from the Tree of Knowledge. They were then driven from Paradise by the angel Michael.

alone do I promise my life and my attempts at peace.

"I have one secret, Elizabeth, a dreadful one. When revealed to you, it will chill you with horror. But you will be far from being surprised at my misery. You will only wonder how I survived what I have endured.

"I will reveal this tale of misery and terror to you the day after our marriage. For, my sweet cousin, there must be no secrets between us. But until then, I beg you not to mention or ask about it. This I most earnestly ask, and I know you will agree."

About a week after the arrival of Elizabeth's letter, we returned to Geneva. The sweet girl welcomed me with warm affection. Yet tears were in her eyes as she looked at my thin frame and feverish cheeks.

I saw a change in her also. She too was thinner. And she had lost much of the heavenly liveliness that had charmed me before. But she still had her gentleness and soft looks of compassion. These made her a more fit companion for one cursed and miserable as I was.

The peace which I now enjoyed didn't last. Memory brought madness with it. And when I thought of what had passed, a real insanity possessed me.

Sometimes I was furious and burned with rage. Sometimes I was low and depressed. I neither spoke nor looked at anyone. I sat motionless, confused by the swarm of miseries that overcame me.

Only Elizabeth had the power to draw me from these fits. Her gentle voice would soothe me when I was moved by passion. And she would inspire me with human feelings when I was numb. She wept with me and for me. When my madness left me, she would reason with me and try to get me to accept everything that had happened.

Ah! It is well for the unfortunate to accept the past. They sometimes find a luxury in expressing terrible grief. But for the guilty there is no such peace. The agonies of remorse poison it.

Soon after my arrival, my father spoke of my immediate marriage with Elizabeth. I remained silent.

"Have you some other attachment, then?" he asked.

"None on earth," I replied. "I love Elizabeth and look forward to our union with delight. Let the day therefore be set. And on that day I will swear myself to my cousin's happiness, in life or death."

"My dear Victor, don't talk like that," said my father. "Much bad luck has fallen on us. But let us only cling closer to what remains. Let us transfer our love for those whom we have lost to those who yet live.

"Our circle will be small. But it will be kept close by the ties of affection and mutual misfortune. Time shall soften your despair. And new and dear objects of care will be born. They will replace those whom we have been so cruelly robbed of."

Such were the lessons of my father. But to me the memory of the threat returned. I thought of how wide-reaching the fiend had yet been in his bloody deeds. Can you wonder I should almost believe nothing could defeat him?

The monster had pronounced those words: *"I shall be with you on your wedding night."* I felt my fate couldn't be avoided. But death was no evil to me compared to the loss of Elizabeth.

I therefore agreed with my father with a satisfied and even cheerful expression. If my cousin agreed, the ceremony should take place in ten days. Thus, I put the seal on my fate, as I thought.

Great God! I didn't imagine for one moment my devilish enemy's actual intention. If I had, I would rather have left my native country forever. I would have wandered a friendless outcast over the earth. But I would never have agreed to this miserable marriage.

But the monster—as if possessed with magic powers—had blinded me to his real intentions. I thought I had prepared only my own death. Instead, I hurried the death of a far dearer victim.

The time set for our marriage drew nearer. Whether from a feeling of cowardice or doom, my heart sank within me. But I hid my feelings under an appearance of gladness. This brought smiles and joy to the faces of my father. But it hardly fooled the ever-watchful and sharper eye of Elizabeth. She looked forward to our union with peaceful contentment mixed with a little fear. For now, we seemed to have found certain and solid happiness. But past misfortunes made her wonder if this might fade into an airy dream. Perhaps soon only deep and everlasting regret would be left.

Preparations were made for the wedding, and congratulatory visits were received. Everyone wore a smiling appearance. In my own heart, I shut up my anxiety as well as I could. I entered with seeming eagerness into my father's plans. But I knew they might only serve as the decorations of my tragedy.

Through my father's efforts, a part of Elizabeth's inheritance had been restored to her by the Austrian government. A small piece of land on the shores of Como belonged to her. It was agreed that we would go to Villa Lavenza immediately after our union. We would spend our first days of happiness beside the beautiful lake near which it stood.

In the meantime, I took great care to defend myself in case the fiend should openly attack me. I constantly carried pistols and a dagger about me. And I was always on the watch for any trick. In this way, I gained a greater peace of mind.

Indeed, as the period approached, the threat appeared more imaginary. I felt it wasn't worthy to disturb my peace. As the day of the wedding drew nearer, happiness appeared more and more certain. It was often spoken of as an occurrence which no accident could possibly prevent.

Elizabeth seemed happy. My quiet behavior greatly helped to calm her mind. But the fateful day arrived. Then she became extremely sad. An expectation of evil swept over her. Perhaps also she thought of the dreadful secret which I had promised to reveal to her on the following day.

In the meantime, my father was overjoyed. In the bustle of preparation, he saw only his niece's low spirits as a bride's shyness.

After the ceremony was performed, a large party gathered at my father's. But it was agreed that Elizabeth and I should begin our journey by water right away. We'd sleep that night at Evian and continue our voyage on the following day. The day was fair and the wind favorable. All smiled on our honeymoon departure.

Those were the last moments of my life when I enjoyed the feeling of happiness. We passed quickly along. The sun was hot, but we were sheltered from its rays by a kind of canopy.[2] Meanwhile, we enjoyed the beauty of the scene.

Sometimes we were on one side of the lake, where we saw Mont Salêve and the pleasant banks of Montalègre. And at a distance, above all else, we saw the beautiful Mont Blanc. A gathering of snowy mountains surrounded her, trying without success to imitate her.

At other times we coasted along the opposite banks. There we saw the dark side of the mighty Jura Mountains. The range formed an almost impassable barrier to any invader who wished to enslave it.

I took Elizabeth's hand.

"You are sorrowful, my love," I said. "Ah! If only you knew what I have suffered and what I may yet go through. You would try to let me taste the quiet and the freedom from despair. At least this one day permits me to enjoy that."

"Be happy, my dear Victor," replied Elizabeth. "There is nothing to distress you, I hope. And be assured that if a lively joy isn't painted in my face, my heart is satisfied. Something whispers to me not to depend too much on the bright future before us. But I won't listen to

---

[2] A canopy is a cloth roof or covering, as over a bed or a boat.

such a **sinister** voice.

"See how fast we move along," she went on. "And see how the clouds make this scene of beauty more interesting. Sometimes they hide and other times they rise above the dome of Mont Blanc.

"Look also at the countless fish that are swimming in the clear waters," she said. "We can make out every pebble that lies at the bottom. What a divine day! How happy and calm all nature appears!"

Thus, Elizabeth tried to keep her thoughts and mine away from all depressing subjects. But her moods often changed. Joy for a few instants shone in her eyes. But it continually gave place to worry and thoughtfulness.

The sun sank lower in the heavens. We passed the river Drance and saw its path through the canyons of the higher hills and the valleys of the lower hills.

Here the Alps come closer to the lake, and we approached a hollow in the mountains which forms its eastern border. The spire of Evian shone under the woods that surrounded it. A range of mountain above mountain overhung the spire.

For a while, the wind carried us along with amazing speed. But it slowed at sunset to a light breeze. The soft air just ruffled the water and caused a pleasant motion among the trees as we approached the shore. The most delightful scent of flowers and hay floated towards us.

The sun sank beneath the horizon as we landed. And as I touched the shore, I felt my cares and fears revive. Soon they were to clasp me and cling to me forever.

Chapter 23

Vocabulary Preview

The following words appear in this chapter. Review the list and get to know the words before you read the chapter.

adversary—enemy; foe
distorted—twisted; misshapen
illuminate—light up; brighten
intimidated—frightened; threatened
jeer—laugh at; make fun of
momentarily—at any time; very soon
tedious—boring; tiresome
tidings—news
wreak—bring about; cause

It was eight o'clock when we landed. We walked for a short time on the shore, enjoying the fleeting light. Then we went on to the inn and looked upon the lovely scene of the waters, woods, and mountains. They were hidden in darkness, yet still displayed their black outlines.

The wind had fallen in the south. Now it rose with great violence in the west. The moon had reached her full height in the heavens and was beginning to descend. The clouds swept across the moon swifter than the flight of the vulture and dimmed her rays.

The lake reflected the scene of the busy heavens. They were made still busier by the restless waves that were beginning to rise. Suddenly a heavy storm of rain descended.

I had been calm during the day. But as soon as night hid the shapes of objects, a thousand fears arose in my mind. I was anxious and watchful. My right hand grasped a pistol which was hidden in my coat.

Every sound terrified me, but I decided that I would stand up for my life. I wouldn't shrink from the conflict until my own life or that of my **adversary** was ended.

For some time, Elizabeth observed my unease in fearful silence. But there was something in my glance that communicated terror to her.

Trembling, she asked, "What is it that upsets you, my dear Victor? What is it you fear?"

"Oh! Peace, peace, my love," replied I. "When this night is over, all will be safe. But this night is dreadful, very dreadful."

I passed an hour in this state of mind. Suddenly, I thought about how fearful the combat I **momentarily** expected would be to my wife. I earnestly begged her to go to bed. I planned not to join her until I had gained some knowledge as to the whereabouts of my enemy.

Elizabeth left me. I continued for some time walking up and down the hallways of the house. I inspected every corner that might offer a hiding place for my adversary. But I discovered no trace of him. I was beginning to suppose that some fortunate thing had happened to prevent his threats from being carried out after all.

Then suddenly I heard a shrill and dreadful scream. It came from the room Elizabeth had disappeared into. As I heard it, the whole truth rushed into my mind. My arms dropped. The motion of every muscle and fiber was frozen. I could feel the blood trickling in my veins and tingling in the farthest parts of my limbs.

This state lasted but for an instant. The scream was repeated, and I rushed into the room.

Great God! Why didn't I die then? Why am I here to tell of the destruction of the best hope and the purest creature of earth? She was there, lifeless and motionless, thrown across the bed. Her head hung down and her pale and **distorted** features were half covered by her hair.

Everywhere I turn I see the same figure. I see her bloodless arms and relaxed form flung by the murderer on the bridal bed. Could I look at this and live?

Alas! Life is stubborn and clings closest where it is most hated. For only a moment I lost consciousness. I fell senseless to the ground.

When I recovered, I found myself surrounded by the people of the inn. Their faces expressed a breathless terror. But the horror of others seemed just a mockery. Their reaction was but a shadow of the feelings that overcame me.

I escaped from them to the room where the body of Elizabeth lay—my life, my wife, so lately living, so dear, so worthy. She had been moved from the position in which I had first found her. Now she lay with her head upon her arm and a handkerchief thrown across her face and neck. I might have supposed her asleep.

I rushed towards her and embraced her with emotion. But the deadly limpness and coldness of the limbs told me that what I now held in my arms was Elizabeth no more. This was not she whom I had loved and cherished. The murderous mark of the fiend's grasp was on her neck. The breath had ceased to arise from her lips.

While I still hung over her in the agony of despair, I happened to look up. The windows of the room had been darkened before. So I felt a kind of panic on seeing the pale yellow light of the moon **illuminate** the room. Then I saw that the shutters had been thrown back.

With a feeling of horror not to be described, I saw at the open window a most hideous and awful figure. A grin was on the monster's face. He seemed to **jeer** as he pointed towards the corpse of my wife with his fiendish finger.

I rushed towards the window and drew a pistol from my bosom. I fired, but he escaped me. He leaped from his place and ran with the swiftness of lightning, plunging into the lake.

The sound of the pistol brought a crowd into the room. I pointed to the spot where he had disappeared, and we followed the track with boats. Nets were cast, but in vain. After several hours we returned, hopeless. Most of my companions believed it had been a form dreamed up in my imagination.

After landing, they went on to search the countryside. Search parties went in different directions among the woods and vines.

I tried to accompany them and went a short distance from the house. But my head whirled round and my steps were like those of a drunken man. I fell at last in a state of total exhaustion. A film covered my eyes, and my skin was dry with fever.

In this condition, I was carried back and placed on a bed. I was hardly aware of what had happened. My eyes wandered round the room as if to seek something that I had lost.

After awhile I arose. As if by instinct, I crawled into the room where the corpse of my beloved lay. There were women weeping around. I hung over it and added my sad tears to theirs.

All this time no clear idea entered my mind. My thoughts rambled over various subjects. I thought with confusion on my misfortunes and their cause. I was bewildered, in a cloud of wonder and horror.

I thought of the death of William, the execution of Justine, the murder of Clerval, and lastly of my wife. Even at that moment, I didn't know whether my only remaining friends were safe from the fiend's cruelty. Even now, my father might be squirming under his grasp. Ernest might be dead at his feet.

This idea made me shudder and spurred me to action. I started up and decided to return to Geneva as quickly as possible.

There were no horses to be found, and I had to return by the lake. But the wind was unfavorable, and the rain fell in torrents. However, it was barely morning. I might reasonably hope to arrive by night.

I hired men to row and took an oar myself. Bodily exercise had always given me relief from mental pain. But now I was extremely upset and felt an overflowing misery. Physical labor was impossible. I threw down the oar and leaned my head upon my hands. I then gave way to every gloomy idea that arose.

If I looked up, I saw scenes that were familiar to me in my happier time. I had gazed upon them just the day before in the company of my wife. Now she was just a shadow and a memory.

Tears streamed from my eyes. The rain had stopped for a moment, and I saw the fish play in the waters as they had done a few hours before. They had then been observed by Elizabeth.

Nothing is so painful to the human mind as a great and sudden change. The sun might shine or the clouds might lower. But nothing could appear to me as it had done the day before. A fiend had snatched every hope of future happiness from me. No creature had ever been so miserable as I was. Such a frightful event is rare in the history of man.

But why should I dwell upon the incidents that followed this last overwhelming event? Mine has been a tale of horrors. I have reached their height, and what I must now relate can only be **tedious** to you.

Know that my friends were snatched away one by one. I was left all alone. My own strength is exhausted. So I must tell in a few words what remains of my hideous story.

I arrived at Geneva. My father and Ernest yet lived, but the former fell under the **tidings** that I bore. I see him now, excellent and respected old man! His eyes wandered emptily, for they had lost their charm and delight— Elizabeth.

Elizabeth was more than his daughter. He loved her with the affection of a man who only has a few years left to live. For that is the time when a man also has few affections left.

Cursed, cursed be the fiend that brought misery on my father's gray hairs and doomed him to waste in misery! He couldn't live under the horrors that were gathered around him. The springs of life suddenly gave way. He was unable to rise from his bed, and in a few days he died in my arms. What then became of me? I don't know. I lost all feeling, and chains and darkness were the only objects that pressed upon me. Sometimes, indeed, I dreamed that I wandered in flowery meadows and pleasant valleys with the friends of my youth. But I awoke and found myself in a dungeon.

Depression followed. But gradually, I understood my miseries and my situation. I was then released from my prison. For they had called me mad. And as I understood, a lonely cell had been my home for many months.

Liberty might have been a useless gift to me. But at the same time that I awakened to sanity, I awoke to revenge. The memory of past misfortunes pressed upon me. I began to think about their cause. This was the monster whom I had created, the miserable demon whom I had sent out into the world for my destruction.

I was possessed by a maddening rage when I thought of him. I desired and eagerly prayed that I might have him within my grasp. I wanted to **wreak** a great and final revenge on his cursed head.

Nor did my hate limit itself to useless wishes for long. I began to consider the best means of capturing him. For this purpose I went to a criminal judge in the town about a month after my release.

I told him that I had an accusation to make. I said I knew the destroyer of my family. And I required the judge to use all of his authority in the capture of the murderer.

The magistrate listened to me with attention and kindness.

"Be assured, sir," said he, "that I shall spare no pains or efforts on my part to find the villain."

"I thank you," replied I. "Therefore, listen to my testimony. It is indeed a tale so strange that I should fear you wouldn't believe it. But there is something in truth which—however amazing—forces one to believe it. The story is too logical to be mistaken for a dream. And I have no reason to lie."

As I addressed him, my manner was impressive but calm. I had formed in my own heart a decision to follow my destroyer to death. This purpose quieted my agony and for a time caused me to accept my life.

I now related my history briefly but also firmly and clearly. I marked the dates with accuracy and never wandered into harsh language or exclamation.

At first the magistrate appeared perfectly unbelieving. But as I continued he became more attentive and interested. I saw him sometimes shudder with horror. At others a lively surprise, unmixed with disbelief, was painted on his face.

At last I had finished my story. I said, "This is the being whom I accuse. I call upon you to use all your power for his capture and punishment. It's your duty as a magistrate. And I believe and hope your feelings as a man won't keep you from doing your duty at this time."

These last words caused a great change in my listener's expression. He had heard my story with a kind of half-belief. It was as if he had been listening to a tale of ghosts and supernatural events. But as a result of this story, he was now called upon to act officially. So he once more became disbelieving.

However, he answered mildly, "I would willingly help you as much as possible in your pursuit. But the creature whom you speak of appears to have powers which would withstand all my best efforts. Who can follow an animal that can travel the sea of ice and live in caves and dens where no man would dare to go?

"Besides," he continued, "some months have gone by since he committed his crimes. No one can guess as to what place he has wandered or where he may now live."

"I'm sure that he lingers near the spot where I live myself," I said. "I doubt he has hidden in the Alps, to be hunted and destroyed like a beast of prey. But I know what you're thinking. You don't believe my story. You don't intend to go after my enemy with the punishment he deserves."

As I spoke, rage sparkled in my eyes. The magistrate was **intimidated.**

"You are mistaken," said he. "I will try. And if it is in my power to capture the monster, be assured that he shall suffer the proper punishment for his crimes.

"But from what you yourself have described to be his abilities, I fear that this will prove impossible. I will go after him in every way I can. But you should prepare to be disappointed."

"That can't be," I said. "But all that I can say will be of little use. My revenge is of no importance to you. I admit it to be a fault. But it is the overwhelming and only passion of my soul. My rage is unspeakable when I remember that the murderer whom I have turned loose upon society still lives.

"You refuse my just demand," I went on. "So I have just one choice. I devote myself to his destruction, either in my life or death."

I trembled with excitement as I said this. There was a wildness in my manner. And I don't doubt there was something of the proud fierceness which the martyrs[1] of old are said to have had.

But the mind of a Genevan magistrate is occupied by far different ideas than those of devotion and heroism. So my actions seemed like madness to him. He tried to soothe me as a nurse does a child. He described my tale as the result of insanity.

"Man," I cried, "how ignorant you are in your pride of wisdom! Stop! You don't know what you're saying."

I ran from the house, angry and disturbed. Then I went away to consider some other plan.

---

[1] Martyrs are people who willingly suffer abuse or death for a cause that's important to them.

Chapter 24

In my present situation, I couldn't think clearly. All my thoughts were swallowed up and lost. I was swept away by fury. Revenge alone gave me strength and self-control. It shaped my feelings and allowed me to be careful and calm. Otherwise, madness or death would have come to me.

My first decision was to leave Geneva forever. When I was happy and beloved, my country was dear to me. Now, in my misfortune, it was hateful. I provided myself with a sum of money, together with a few jewels which had belonged to my mother. Then I left.

And now my wanderings began which are to end only with death. I have traveled a great part of the earth. I have endured all the hardships which travelers in deserts and uncivilized countries are likely to meet.

How I have lived I hardly know. Many times I

stretched my failing limbs upon the sandy plain and prayed for death. But revenge kept me alive. I didn't dare die and leave my adversary alive.

When I left Geneva, my first task was to trace the steps of my fiendish enemy. So I began to search for some clue. But my plan wasn't organized, and I wandered many hours round the borders of the town. I couldn't decide which path to take.

Night came. I found myself at the entrance of the cemetery where William, Elizabeth, and my father rested. I entered it and approached the tomb which marked their graves.

Everything was silent except the leaves of the trees, which were gently stirred by the wind. The night was nearly dark. The scene would have been solemn and moving even to an uninterested observer. The spirits of the dead seemed to dart around and to cast a shadow. I felt the shadow but couldn't see it.

The deep grief I first felt here quickly changed to rage and despair. They were dead and I lived. Their murderer also lived. And to destroy him I must drag out my weary life.

I knelt on the grass and kissed the earth. With quivering lips I exclaimed, "By the sacred earth on which I kneel, by the spirits that wander near me, by the deep and everlasting grief I feel, I swear. And by you, oh Night, and the spirits that watch over you, I swear. I swear to go after the demon who caused this misery. And I will hunt him until he or I shall perish in mortal conflict.

"For this purpose I will preserve my life. Only to carry out this dear revenge will I again look at the sun and walk on the greenness of the earth. Otherwise, these should vanish from my eyes forever.

"And I call on you, spirits of the dead, and on you, wandering servants of revenge. I need you to help me and guide me in my work. Let the cursed and hellish monster drink deep of agony. Let him feel the despair that now torments me."

I had begun my prayer with solemnity and awe. I felt almost assured that the ghosts of my murdered friends heard and approved my wishes. But the furies[1] possessed me as I finished. Rage choked my words.

In the stillness of the night, I was answered by a loud and fiendish laugh. It rang on my ears long and heavily. The mountains re-echoed with it. I felt as if all hell surrounded me with mockery and laughter.

Surely in that moment I should have been possessed by wildness and destroyed my miserable life. But my vow was heard and I was devoted to revenge.

The laughter died away. Then a well-known and hated voice—apparently close to my ear—addressed me in a loud whisper.

"I'm satisfied, miserable wretch!" he said. "You have decided to live, and I'm satisfied."

I darted towards the spot from which the sound came. But the devil escaped my grasp. Suddenly the broad disk of the moon arose. It shone full upon his ghastly and twisted shape. I watched as he fled with more than human speed.

I chased him, and for many months this has been my task. Guided by a slight clue, I followed the windings of the Rhone, but in vain. The blue Mediterranean appeared. And one night, by accident, I spotted the fiend hiding himself in a ship. He was bound for the Black Sea.[2] I took my passage in the same ship, but he escaped. I don't know how.

He escaped me among the wilds of Tartary[3] and Russia. Still I have always followed in his track. Sometimes the peasants—frightened by this horrid being—told me which way he went. Sometimes he himself feared that I'd lose all trace of

---

[1] In ancient Greek mythology, furies are spirits who punished others by torturing them with feelings of guilt.

[2] The Mediterranean Sea is a great body of water extending across the southern part of Europe. The Black Sea lies to the east of it.

[3] Tartary is the homeland in eastern Europe and northwest Asia of Muslim and Turkish people known as Tartars.

him and give up and die. So he left some clue to guide me. The snows fell on my head, and I saw the print of his huge step on the white plain.

You are first entering on life. Care is new and agony unknown to you. How can you understand what I have felt and still feel? Cold, want, and exhaustion were the least pains which I was forced to endure.

I was cursed by some devil. I carried about with me my eternal hell. Yet still, a spirit of good followed and guided me. When I was about to lose all hope, it was there. It would pull me away from what seemed to be impossible difficulties.

Sometimes my body was overcome by hunger. It sank under the exhaustion. But then I would find a meal prepared for me in the desert. The food was indeed coarse like that of the peasants. But the meal filled me and raised my spirits. And I won't doubt it was put there by the spirits that I had begged to help me.

Sometimes all was dry, the heavens cloudless, and I was parched with thirst. But then a small cloud would darken the sky, shed the few drops that revived me, and vanish.

When I could, I followed the courses of rivers. But the demon generally avoided these. It was here that the main population of the country lived. In other places human beings were seldom seen. So I generally lived off the wild animals that crossed my path.

I had money with me and gained the friendship of the villagers by offering it. Or I brought with me some food that I had killed. I would take a small part of it for myself. Then I always presented the rest to those who had provided me with fire and tools for cooking.

The way I lived my life was indeed hateful to me. It was only during sleep that I felt joy. Oh, blessed sleep! Often, when most miserable, I sank to rest, and my dreams relaxed me even to delight.

The spirits that guarded me had provided these moments—or rather hours—of happiness. For I needed my strength to complete my journey. I should have sunk under my hardships if I hadn't been allowed this relief. During the day, the hope of night kept my spirits up. For in sleep I saw my friends, my wife, and my beloved country. Again I saw the kindly face of my father. I heard the silver tones of my Elizabeth's voice. I saw Clerval enjoying health and youth.

Often I became wearied by a difficult march. So I'd persuade myself that I was dreaming until night should come. Then I should enjoy reality in the arms of my dearest friends.

What a painful fondness I felt for them! Sometimes they haunted even my waking hours. How I clung to their dear forms and persuaded myself that they still lived!

At such moments, the revenge that burned within me died in my heart. I chased the demon more as a task given by heaven. It seemed the mechanical impulse of some power that I was wasn't aware of. It was no longer the feverish desire of my soul.

What the monster's feelings were I don't know. However, sometimes he left marks in writing on the barks of trees or cut in stone. They guided me and stirred my fury.

These words were **legible** in one of these writings:

"My reign is not yet over. You live, and my power is complete. Follow me. I seek the everlasting ices of the north. There you will feel the misery of cold and frost, which don't affect me. If you don't follow too slowly, you'll find a dead hare near here. Eat and be refreshed.

"Come on, my enemy. We have yet to wrestle for our lives. But you must survive many hard and miserable hours until that time shall arrive."

Mocking devil! Again do I vow revenge. Again do I condemn you to torture and death, miserable fiend. I will never give up my search until he or I perish. Then with what delight shall I join my Elizabeth and my departed friends. Even now they prepare for me the reward of my tiresome work and horrible travels!

So I still continued my journey northward. The snows thickened, and the cold became almost too bitter to endure. The peasants were shut up in their huts. Only a few of the most hardy came outside. But they only seized the starving animals forced from their hiding places to seek food. The rivers were covered with ice, and no fish could be caught. And thus I was cut off from my chief source of food.

My enemy's triumph increased with the difficulty of my labors. One note that he left was in these words: "Prepare! Your struggles only begin. Wrap yourself in furs and gather food. For we shall soon enter upon a journey where your sufferings will satisfy my everlasting hatred."

My courage and **perseverance** increased at these mocking words. I decided not to fail in my purpose, and I called on heaven to support me. Then I continued with endless determination to travel great deserts. At last the ocean appeared at a distance and formed most of the horizon border.

Oh! How different it was from the blue waters of the south. This sea was covered with ice. I could only tell it apart from the land by its great wildness and unevenness.

Long ago, the Greeks wept for joy when they looked upon the Mediterranean from the hills of Asia. They greeted the end of their travels with delight. I didn't weep, but I knelt down. With a full heart I thanked my guiding spirit for leading me to this place in safety. There I hoped—in spite of my adversary's mockery—to meet and battle with him.

Some weeks before this period, I had gotten a sledge and dogs. I thus traveled the snows with unbelievable speed.

I didn't know whether the fiend had the same advantages. However, before this I had daily lost ground in the chase. But I now gained on him. I gained so much that when I first saw the ocean he was only one day's journey ahead of me. I hoped to stop him before he reached the beach. Therefore, I pressed on with new courage. And in two days I arrived at a poor village on the seashore.

I asked the villagers about the fiend and gained correct information. A gigantic monster, they said, had arrived the night before. He was armed with a gun and many pistols. He had scared away the inhabitants of a lonely cottage by his terrible appearance. Then he had carried off their store of winter food and placed it in a sledge.

He had seized a number of trained dogs and harnessed them to the sledge. The same night—to the joy of the horror-struck villagers—he had taken off on his journey across the sea. The direction he headed for led to no land. And they guessed that he must quickly be destroyed by the breaking of the ice. Or at least he'd be frozen by the eternal frosts.

On hearing this information, I suffered a temporary return of despair. He had escaped me. Now I must begin a deadly and almost endless journey across the mountainous ices of the ocean. I must go into a cold that few people could endure for long. I was used to a pleasant and sunny climate. I couldn't hope to survive this.

Yet I remembered that the fiend might live and be triumphant. Then my rage and desire for revenge returned. Like a mighty tide, they overwhelmed every other feeling. I took a short rest. The spirits of the dead stayed near and urged me to get on with my revenge. When I was refreshed, I prepared for my journey.

I traded my land-sledge for one suitable for the rough surface of the frozen ocean. Then I purchased a plentiful stock of supplies and departed from land.

I can't guess how many days have passed since then. But I have suffered great misery. Only the eternal desire burning within my heart—the desire for a just revenge— could have enabled me to survive.

Huge, jagged mountains of ice often blocked my way. I often heard the thunder of the ground sea, which threatened to destroy me. But again the frost came and made the paths of the sea secure.

By the amount of food which I had eaten, I should guess that I had spent three weeks in this journey. I forced myself to keep hopeful. But bitter drops of despair and grief often fell from my eyes.

Once, the poor animals that carried me had—with incredible effort—reached the top of a sloping ice mountain. One died from exhaustion. I viewed the space before me with anguish. Then suddenly my eye caught sight of a dark speck upon the dim plain.

I strained my sight to discover what it could be. I uttered a wild cry of joy when I saw a sledge. Within it was a misshapen, well-known form.

Oh! Hope returned to my heart with such a burning gush! Warm tears filled my eyes. But I quickly wiped them away so they wouldn't blur the view I had of the demon. Still, my sight was dimmed by the burning drops. At last, I gave way to the emotions that overwhelmed me, and I wept aloud.

But this was no time for delay. I freed the dogs of their dead companion and gave them a large portion of food. I rested for an hour. This was absolutely necessary and yet also bitterly unpleasant to me. I then continued my route.

The sledge was still visible. I didn't lose sight of it again except for short moments. At times some large ice-rock hid it. But indeed, I could tell that I gained on it. I journeyed in this way for two days. At last, I saw my enemy no more than a mile away. My heart leaped within me.

I seemed almost within reach of my foe. But my hopes were suddenly dashed. I lost all trace of him more completely than I had ever done before.

I heard the ground sea, and the waters rolled and swelled beneath me. The thunder of the ground sea's movement became more terrible every moment. I pressed on, but in vain. The wind arose, and the sea roared. Like the mighty shock of an earthquake, it split and cracked with a tremendous and overwhelming sound. The work was soon finished. In a few minutes, a violent sea rolled between me and my enemy. I was left drifting on a scattered piece of ice that was becoming smaller every moment. I was being prepared for a horrible death.

In this manner many alarming hours passed. Several of my dogs died. And I myself was about to sink under the burden of distress. But then I saw your ship riding at anchor. You were my hope for relief and life.

I had no idea that ships ever came so far north. So I was amazed at the sight. I quickly destroyed part of my sledge and made some oars. By these means I was able, with endless exhaustion, to move my ice raft toward your ship.

I had decided what to do if you were going southwards. I would still trust myself to the mercy of the seas rather than give up my goal. I hoped to persuade you to give me a boat with which I could go after my enemy.

But your direction was northwards. You took me on board when my strength was exhausted. I should soon have sunk under my many hardships into a death which I still dread. For my task is not complete.

Oh! When will my guiding spirit lead me to the demon? When will it allow me the rest I so much desire? Or must I die, and he yet live? If I do, Walton, swear to me that he shall not escape. Swear that you will seek him and satisfy my revenge in his death.

And do I dare to ask of you to take on my mission? To endure the hardships that I have undergone? No. I'm not so selfish. Yet he may appear after I'm dead. If so, swear that he shall not triumph over my many woes. Swear that he won't survive and add to the list of his dark crimes.

His words are forceful and persuasive. And once, they

even had power over my heart. But don't trust him. His soul is as hellish as his form, full of evil and fiendlike cruelty.

Don't listen to him. Call on the names of William, Justine, Clerval, Elizabeth, my father, and the wretched Victor. Thrust your sword into his heart. I will linger near and direct the steel to the right place.

Walton, continuing.

August 26th, 17—

You have read this strange and terrific story, Margaret. Do you not feel your blood curdle with horror, as even now my own blood does?

Sometimes, seized with sudden agony, he couldn't continue his tale. At others, his voice was broken, yet sharp. He spoke with difficulty those words so full of pain.

His fine and lovely eyes sometimes lit up with anger. Other times they became dull with sorrow and misery.

Sometimes he was in control of his voice and expression. Then he'd describe the most horrible incidents calmly, with no hint of being upset. Then—like a volcano bursting forth—his face would suddenly change. He would take on an expression of the wildest rage as he shrieked out curses on his adversary.

His tale is logical and told with an appearance of the simplest truth. He also showed me the letters of Felix and Safie. And I did see the monster's form from our ship. I must admit that these made me believe the truth of his story even more than his own words. However, he did speak sincerely and believably.

Such a monster really exists, then! I can't doubt it, yet I am lost in surprise and wonder. Sometimes I tried to discover exactly how Frankenstein made the creature. But on this point he wouldn't speak.

"Are you mad, my friend?" said he. "Or where does your senseless curiosity lead you? Would you also create a devilish enemy for yourself and the world? Peace, peace! Learn from my miseries and don't seek to increase your own."

Frankenstein discovered that I made notes concerning his history. He asked to see them. Then he himself corrected and added to them in many places. Mainly, he added life and spirit to the conversations he held with his enemy.

"You have recorded my story," said he. "I wouldn't want for future generations to get any mistaken facts."

Thus has a week passed by while I listened to the strangest tale that imagination ever formed. My thoughts and every feeling of my soul have been drunk up by interest in my guest. His tale and his own fine and gentle manners have fascinated me.

I wish to soothe him. Yet can I advise anyone so miserable and despairing to live? Oh, no! The only joy that he can now know will be when his shattered spirit is quieted by peace and death.

Yet he enjoys one comfort, the result of delirium[4] and loneliness. He believes that his dreams are real. In them he speaks with his friends. And from these conversations he gains comfort for his misery or excitement for revenge.

He believes his friends aren't the creations of his fancy, but the beings themselves. He believes they visit him from the regions of a faraway world. This faith gives a seriousness to his words. To me, they become almost as striking and interesting as the truth.

Our conversations aren't always about his own history and misfortunes. He shows great knowledge and quick and sharp understanding of general literature. He has a way with words that is strong and touching. And he often relates a sorrowful incident that stirs the feelings of pity or love. When he does, I can't listen to him without tears.

[4] Delirium is a mental disturbance or confusion caused by shock or high fever.

What a glorious creature he must have been in his better days! Even in his ruin he is noble and godlike. He seems to feel his own worth and the greatness of his fall.

"When younger," said he, "I believed myself destined for some great deeds. My feelings are deep, but I had the good judgment I needed for high achievements.

"This feeling of my worth supported me when others would have felt defeated. For I thought it criminal to throw away my talents in useless grief. These talents might be useful to my fellow creatures.

"I thought about the work I had completed—indeed, nothing less than the creation of a sensitive and thinking animal. I couldn't rank myself with the crowd of common dreamers.

"This thought supported me at the beginning of my career," he said. "But now it serves only to plunge me lower in the dust. All my ambitions and hopes mean nothing. Like the angel who wanted to be godlike, I am chained in an eternal hell.

"My imagination was **vivid**, yet my powers of thought and discipline were sharp. By combining these qualities, I came up with the idea and carried out the creation of a man.

"Even now, I can't remember without emotion the thoughts I had as I worked. I trod heaven in my thoughts, now rejoicing in my powers, now burning with the idea of their results. From my childhood I was full of high hopes and ambition. But how I am sunk!

"Oh!" he cried. "My friend, if you had known me as I once was! You wouldn't recognize me in this shameful state. Depression rarely visited my heart. A high destiny seemed to bear me on. But at last I fell, never, never again to rise." He paused.

Margaret, must I then lose this fine being? I have longed for a friend. I have looked for one who would sympathize with and love me. Behold, on these desert seas I have found such a one. But I fear I have gained him only to realize his value and then lose him. I'd persuade him to accept life, but he hates the idea.

"Walton," he said, "I thank you for your kind intentions towards such a miserable wretch. You speak of new ties and fresh affections. But do you think that any can replace those that are gone?

"Can any man be to me as Clerval was, or any woman another Elizabeth? Our childhood companions always know us in a certain way. A later friend doesn't have this power.

"Our early companions know our childhood moods," he went on. "These moods may change over time, but they're never erased. And such companions can judge our motives better. They understand why we think the way we do.

"A sister or a brother can never suspect the other of fraud or false dealing. At least not unless such actions have been shown early. But another friend may be suspicious in spite of himself. It doesn't matter how strong the friendship is.

"But I enjoyed friends who were dear not only through habit and togetherness," he said. "It was for their own worth as well. And wherever I am, I shall hear the soothing voice of my Elizabeth and the words of Clerval. They will be always whispered in my ear.

"They are dead. And only one feeling in my loneliness can persuade me to preserve my life. That is if I were engaged in any great undertaking or plan. It would have to be of great use to my fellow creatures. Then I could live to fulfill my work.

"But that is not my destiny. I must hunt and destroy the being to whom I gave life. Then my time on earth will be complete, and I may die."

September 2nd

My beloved Sister,

I write to you surrounded by danger. I have no idea whether I will ever again see dear England and the dearer friends that live there.

I am enclosed by mountains of ice which allow no escape. They threaten at every moment to crush my ship. The brave fellows who agreed to be my companions look towards me for aid. But I have none to give. There is something terribly alarming in our situation. Yet my courage and hopes haven't left me. However, it is terrible to consider that these men's lives are endangered because of me. If we are lost, my mad plans are the cause.

And what will be the state of your mind, Margaret? You won't hear of my destruction. So you will anxiously await my return. Years will pass, and you will have times of despair and yet be tortured by hope.

Oh! My beloved sister. I am sickened to think I might fail you. That would be more terrible to me than my own death. But you have a husband and lovely children. You may be happy. Heaven bless you and make you so!

My unfortunate guest views me with the tenderest compassion. He tries to fill me with hope. He talks as if life were something he valued.

He reminds me of how often the same accidents have happened to other sailors who tried to sail this sea. And in spite of myself, he makes me feel cheerful about the outcome.

Even the sailors feel the power of his words. When he speaks, they no longer despair. He raises their spirits. And while they listen to him, they believe these huge mountains of ice are mole-hills. They feel they can overcome any differences.

These feelings won't last. Each day we remain trapped fills them with fear. I almost dread a mutiny[5] caused by this despair.

September 5th

A scene of such unusual interest has occurred that I feel I must record it. Though it's very unlikely that these papers may ever reach you.

We are still surrounded by mountains of ice. And

---

[5] A mutiny is a revolt against those in charge.

we're still in terrible danger of being crushed in their movement. The cold is **excessive**. And many of my unfortunate companions have already found a grave in this deserted region.

Frankenstein's health has gotten worse daily. A feverish fire still glimmers in his eyes, but he is exhausted. Sometimes he suddenly gains some energy. But he quickly sinks again into apparent lifelessness.

I mentioned in my last letter that I feared a possible mutiny. This morning I was roused by half a dozen of the sailors. They demanded entrance into the cabin. At the time, I was watching my pale friend. His eyes were half closed and his arms and legs were unmoving.

The sailors entered, and their leader addressed me. He told me that he and his companions had been chosen by the other sailors. They had come to me to make me a request which—in all fairness, they said—I couldn't refuse.

They noted that we were trapped in ice and should probably never escape. But they imagined that the ice might break up and a free passage be opened. If so, they feared that I should be **rash** enough to continue my voyage. Might I not lead them into fresh dangers when they might have escaped?

Therefore, they insisted that I should make them a solemn promise. If the ship were ever freed I would instantly turn southwards.

This speech troubled me. I hadn't lost hope yet. I hadn't even thought of returning if we were set free. Yet could I—in justice, or even in possibility—refuse this demand? I hesitated before I answered.

Frankenstein had at first been silent. Indeed, he hardly seemed to have strength enough to listen. But now he roused himself. His eyes sparkled, and his cheeks flushed with brief energy.

Turning towards the men, he said, "What do you mean? What do you demand of your captain? Are you so easily turned from your plan, then? Didn't you call this a glorious voyage? And why was it glorious?

"Not because the way was smooth and peaceful as a southern sea. But because it was full of dangers and terror. Because at every new incident, you had to call on all your determination and show your courage. Because danger and death surrounded it, and these you were to brave and overcome.

"For these reasons it was a glorious and honorable undertaking," Frankenstein went on. "You were hereafter to be famous as helping the human race. Your names would be adored as belonging to brave men who died for honor and the benefit of mankind.

"And now, look! You have met the first possibility of danger. Or, if you will, the first mighty and terrific trial of your courage. And you shrink away.

"You are content to be handed down as men who didn't have enough strength to endure cold and danger. And so, poor souls, you were chilly and returned to your warm firesides.

"Why, that didn't require all this preparation. You didn't have to come this far and drag your captain to the shame of a defeat. For all you're doing is proving yourselves cowards.

"Oh! Be men, or be more than men. Be as firm as a rock in your goals. This ice isn't made of what your hearts should be. Ice is changeable. It can't defeat you if you say that it can't.

"Don't return to your families with the mark of disgrace on your heads," my friend continued. "Return as heroes who have fought and conquered. Heroes who don't know what it is to turn their backs on the foe."

He spoke in a tone that perfectly expressed his feelings. His eyes were full of great plans and heroism. Can you wonder that these men were moved? They looked at one another and were unable to reply.

I spoke. I told them to leave and consider what had been said. I said I wouldn't lead them farther north if they deeply wished for me not to. But I said that I hoped that—after thinking it over—their courage would return. They left, and I turned towards my friend. But he was sunk in weakness and seemed almost lifeless. How will all this end? I don't know. But I would rather die than return shamefully, with my goal not accomplished. Yet I fear such will be my fate. The men aren't held up by ideas of glory and honor. So they can never willingly continue to endure their present hardships.

September 7th

The deed is done. I have agreed to return if we are not destroyed. Thus my hopes are dashed by cowardice and indecision. I will come back ignorant and disappointed. It requires more self-control than I have to bear this injustice with patience.

September 12th

It is over. I am returning to England. I have lost my hopes of useful deeds and glory. I have lost my friend. But I will try to describe these bitter happenings to you, my dear sister. And while I am floating towards England and towards you, I won't lose heart.

On September 9th, the ice began to move. Roarings like thunder were heard from far away as the islands split and cracked in every direction. We were in danger, but we could only remain still. So I focused my attention on my unfortunate guest. His illness had increased to the point that he was kept entirely to his bed.

The ice cracked behind us and was driven with force towards the north. A breeze sprang from the west. And on the 11th, the passage towards the south became perfectly free.

The sailors saw this. Their return to their native country was apparently assured. A shout of wild joy broke from them, loud and long-continued. Frankenstein, who was dozing, awoke and asked what the noise was about.

"They shout," I said, "because they will soon return to England."

"Will you really return, then?"

"Alas, yes!" I said. "I can't deny their demands. I can't lead them unwillingly to danger, and I must return."

"Do so, if you will," he said. "But I won't. You may give up your purpose, but mine is assigned to me by heaven. I dare not. I am weak, but I have spirits to help me in my revenge. Surely they will give me strength enough."

Saying this, he tried to spring from the bed. But the effort was too great for him. He fell back and fainted.

It was long before he recovered. I often thought that life was entirely gone. At last he opened his eyes. He breathed with difficulty and was unable to speak.

The doctor gave him a drink to settle him and ordered us not to disturb him. It the meantime, he told me that my friend certainly didn't have many hours to live.

His judgment was given, and I could only grieve and be patient. I sat by his bed, watching him. His eyes were closed, and I thought he slept. But soon he called to me in a weak voice. He asked me to come near.

"Alas!" he said. "The strength I depended on is gone. I feel that I shall soon die. And he—my enemy and torturer—may still live. Walton, don't think that in the last moments of my life I feel that burning hatred. I don't feel the strong desire of revenge I once had. But I feel myself justified in wanting the death of my enemy.

"During these last days I have been busy examining my past conduct. Nor do I find it at fault. In a fit of enthusiastic madness I created a thinking creature. As his maker, I felt I had to assure his happiness and well-being the best I could.

"This was my duty, but there was another still greater than that. My duties towards mankind had more right to my attention. For I had to think of the happiness of a lot of people as opposed to one creature of my making.

Urged by this view, I refused to create a companion for the first creature. And I did right in refusing.

"He showed extreme cruelty and selfishness in evil," Frankenstein continued. "He destroyed my friends. He murdered beings who had fine feelings, happiness, and wisdom. Nor do I know where his thirst for revenge may end.

"He'd be miserable if he couldn't cause more evil. So he ought to die. The task of his destruction was mine, but I have failed. I once asked you to take on my unfinished work. I did so when driven by selfish and vicious motives. And I renew this request now, this time only out of reason and virtue.

"Yet I can't ask you to forget your country and friends to fulfill this task. And now you are returning to England. You will have little chance of meeting with him.

"But consider the points I have made. Think of your duties and decide what is more important. I leave it to you. My judgment and ideas are already disturbed by my near death. I don't dare ask you to do what I think right, for my feelings may still be guided by passion.

"That the fiend should live to be a tool of mischief disturbs me. On the other hand, this hour is the only happy one which I have enjoyed for several years. This is because I soon expect my release. The forms of the beloved dead dart before me, and I hurry to their arms.

"Farewell, Walton! Seek happiness in peace. Avoid ambition—even if it's only the seemingly innocent ambition of becoming known in science and discoveries. Yet why do I say this? My own hopes in this have been dashed. Maybe another will succeed."

His voice became fainter as he spoke. At last—exhausted by his effort—he sank into silence. About half an hour afterwards, he tried again to speak but was unable. He pressed my hand weakly, and his eyes closed forever. The gleam of a gentle smile passed away from his lips.

Margaret, what comment can I make on the quick

death of this glorious spirit? What can I say that will enable you to understand my deep sorrow? All that I should express would be useless and weak.

My tears flow. My mind is overshadowed by a cloud of disappointment. But I journey towards England, and I may there find comfort.

I am interrupted. What are those sounds I hear? It is midnight. The breeze blows fairly, and the guards on deck barely stir. Again there is a sound like a human voice, but hoarser. It comes from the cabin where the remains of Frankenstein still lie. I must arise and examine. Good night, my sister.

Great God! What a scene has just taken place! I am still dizzy just remembering it. I hardly know whether I shall have the power to describe it. Yet the tale which I have already told would be incomplete without this final and remarkable **catastrophe.**

I entered the cabin where the remains of my ill-fated and admirable friend lay. Over him hung a form which I cannot find words to describe. It was gigantic in size, yet rough and twisted in its build.

As he hung over the coffin, his face was hidden by long locks of ragged hair. But one huge hand was held out. It was like the hand of a mummy.

He heard me approach. He then stopped his exclamations of grief and horror and sprang towards the window. Never have I seen such a horrible vision as his face. It was of the most extreme ugliness.

Without thinking, I shut my eyes. I tried to remember what my duties were with regard to this destroyer. Then I called on him to stay.

He paused and looked on me with wonder. Again he turned towards the lifeless form of his creator, seeming to forget my presence. Every look and movement seemed caused by the wildest rage of some uncontrollable passion.

"That is also my victim!" he exclaimed. "In his murder my crimes are complete. This miserable part of my life is drawing to a close! Oh, Frankenstein! Generous and unselfish being! What does it matter that I now ask you to pardon me? I have completely destroyed you by destroying all you loved. Alas! He is cold. He cannot answer me."

His voice seemed smothered. My first impulses had been to obey my friend's dying request and destroy his enemy. But now I was held back by a mixture of curiosity and compassion.

I approached this tremendous being. I didn't dare raise my eyes to his face again. There was something utterly frightening and unearthly in his ugliness. I tried to speak, but the words died away on my lips.

The monster continued his wild and meaningless words of self-blame. When he paused in his exclamations, I at last gathered the courage to speak.

"Your regret is now pointless," I said. "You should have listened to the voice of conscience earlier. You should have paid attention to the stings of sorrow before you let your evil revenge go this far. If you had, Frankenstein would still be alive."

"And do you dream?" said the demon. "Do you think that I was then dead to agony and regret?"

He pointed at the corpse and said, "He didn't suffer when the act was completed. Oh! He didn't suffer one ten-thousandth of the anguish I felt all this time. A frightful selfishness hurried me on. But my heart was poisoned with sorrow.

"Do you think that Clerval's groans were music to my ears? My heart was made to enjoy love and sympathy. Then it was wrenched by misery to evil and hatred. It didn't endure the violence of the change without torture. You can't even imagine the torture I've been through.

"After Clerval's murder I returned to Switzerland. I was heart-broken and overcome with pain. I pitied Frankenstein, and my pity amounted to horror. I hated myself.

"But then I discovered that my creator dared to hope

for happiness," the monster continued. "He—the cause of my life and of its unspeakable torture! He piled misery and despair upon me, but sought his own enjoyment. He could take part in feelings and passions which I was forever denied.

"Helpless envy and bitter rage filled me with a thirst for revenge that wouldn't go away. I remembered my threat and decided it should be carried out. I knew that I was preparing a deadly torture for myself. But I was the slave, not the master. I hated the impulse, but I couldn't disobey.

"Yet when she died! No, then I wasn't miserable. I had cast off all feeling and kept down all anguish. My despair took over my actions. From that time on, evil became my good. Urged this far, I had no choice. I had to change my nature to fit the choices I had willingly made.

"Completing my devilish plans became a passion that couldn't be satisfied. And now it is ended. There is my last victim!"

I was at first touched by the misery he showed. But then I remembered what Frankenstein had said of the being's powerful speech and persuasion. And then I again looked at the lifeless form of my friend. Rage was reawakened within me.

"Wretch!" I said. "It is well that you come here to whine over the ruin you have caused. You throw a torch into a pile of buildings. And when they are burned, you sit among the ruins and grieve about it.

"**Hypocritical** fiend!" I continued. "What if the one you mourn still lived? He'd still be the object of your cursed revenge. It isn't pity that you feel. You're sorry only because the victim of your cruelty is taken from your power."

"Oh, that isn't it—that isn't it," interrupted the being. "Yet such must be the way you have been made to see it. To you, that must appear to be the reason for my actions. Yet I don't seek someone to understand my misery. I may never find sympathy.

"Once I looked for it. And my whole being overflowed with the love of goodness, the feelings of happiness and affection. I wanted to take part in all this. "But now goodness has become a shadow to me. And happiness and affection are turned into bitter and cruel despair. Where should I go for sympathy? I am content to suffer alone as long my sufferings last. When I die, I am well satisfied I will be remembered only with disgust.

"Once, my imagination was soothed with dreams of goodness, of fame, and of enjoyment," he continued. "Once I falsely hoped to meet with beings who excused my outward appearance. They would love me for the excellent qualities which I was capable of showing. I fed on high thoughts of honor and devotion.

"But now, crime has brought me below the meanest animal. No guilt, no mischief, no cruelty, no misery can be found even close to mine. Sometimes I run over the frightful list of my sins. I can't believe I'm the same creature who once thought only of the beauty of goodness.

"But it is even so. The fallen angel becomes a cruel devil. Yet even that enemy of God and man had friends and companions with him in his ruin. I am alone.

"You call Frankenstein your friend," said the monster. "You seem to have a knowledge of my crimes and his misfortunes. But how many of the details could he tell you? He couldn't sum up the hours and months of misery which I spent in useless passions.

"For while I destroyed his hopes, I didn't satisfy my own desires. They were forever strong and hungry. Still I desired love and fellowship, yet I was cast away.

"Was there no unfairness in this? Am I to be thought the only criminal, when all humankind sinned against me? Why don't you hate Felix, who drove me—his friend—from his door with disgrace? Why don't you insult the farmer who sought to destroy the one who saved his child?

"Nay, these are good and perfect beings!" he said. "I,

the miserable and the abandoned, am a monster. I am to be rejected, and kicked, and trampled on. Even now my blood boils at the memory of this injustice.

"But it's true that I am a wretch. I have murdered the lovely and the helpless. I have strangled the innocent as they slept. I have choked to death the throat of one who never injured me or any other living thing.

"My creator was the perfect example of all that is worthy of love and admiration among men. But I have brought him to misery. I have pushed him even to that final ruin. There he lies, white and cold in death.

"You hate me, but your hatred can't equal the hatred I feel for myself," said the demon. "I look on my hands, which performed the deed. I think of my heart, which thought of the deed. And I long for the moment when I can look at my hands and those horrible thoughts will stop haunting me.

"Don't fear that I shall cause any future mischief. My work is nearly complete. Neither yours nor any man's death is needed to complete the purpose of my being and do what must be done. But it requires my own death.

"Don't think that I shall be slow to perform this sacrifice. I shall leave your ship on the ice raft which brought me here. And I shall seek the most northern part of the globe.

"I shall collect my funeral pile and burn my miserable body to ashes. My remains shall offer no clue to any curious and wicked wretch who would create another like me.

"I shall die," he said. "I shall no longer feel the agonies I am now filled with. I shall not be owned by those feelings which are still unsatisfied. The one who called me to life is dead. And when I shall live no more, the very memory of us both will quickly vanish.

"I shall no longer see the sun or stars or feel the winds play on my cheeks. Light, feeling, and sense will pass away. And in this condition must I find my happiness.

"Some years ago the sights of the world were first

opened to me," he said. "Then, I felt the cheering warmth of summer. I heard the rustling of the leaves and the songs of the birds. When these were all I knew, I should have wept to die. Now, death is my only comfort. I am ruined by crimes and torn by the bitterest regret. Where can I find rest except in death?

"Farewell! I leave you. You are the last of humankind whom these eyes will ever see.

"Farewell, Frankenstein!" he continued. "If you were still alive, you would still cherish a desire of revenge against me. Your revenge would be better satisfied by making me live rather than causing my death.

"But it wasn't so. You did seek my death so that I wouldn't cause greater misery. Perhaps yet—in some way unknown to me—you haven't stopped thinking and feeling. If so, you wouldn't desire against me a revenge greater than what I feel.

"Cursed as you were, my agony was still greater than yours. For the bitter sting of sorrow and regret will never stop torturing me—not until death shall end it forever.

"But soon I shall die," he cried with sad and solemn enthusiasm. And what I now feel will be no longer felt. Soon these burning miseries will be gone. I shall climb my funeral pile in triumph. I shall rejoice in the pain of the torturing flames.

"The light of that blaze will fade away. My ashes will be swept into the sea by the winds. My spirit will sleep in peace. Or if it thinks, it won't think like this. Farewell."

He sprang from the cabin window as he said this. Then he fell to the ice raft which lay close to the ship. He was soon carried away by the waves and lost in darkness and distance.